STONED IN THE AFTERLIFE:

Stoned In The Afterlife:

A Possible Journey, Part One

RUPERT RUSSEL DOUGLAS

SITA Publishing House

Contents

ISBN: 978-1-7397071-2-5.

First Printing, 2022

To AW,
I miss everything about you.

Chapter 1

The day was warming with the last of the summer sun, under a cloudless blue sky. Joe wasn't interested in the sky he was more interested in the tickling sensation under his left buttock. The feeling had bothered him for the last few corners. Something small pressed against him and he wriggled to shift the cause of his discomfort. He completely lost all concentration when, as he approached a T-junction, the sudden sharp pain caused by the sting of the wasp that had found itself mysteriously stuck in the gap between the back and the base of his car seat, made him thrust his hips forward, straightening his body. His right foot pressed down hard on the accelerator, causing the motor to turn at revolutions that the car had only ever experienced during its journey from the showroom to Joe's house, whilst being driven by the young man charged with delivering it.

Joe was thrust towards the entrance opposite, at the point of the T-junction, of a scrapyard. He never made it to the entrance, he shot onto the path of an articulated lorry, which had managed to maintain its speed as the lights had changed, which then bent and crushed and threw his car across the pavement into the wall of the scrapyard.

Joe knew very little of the accident when he opened his eyes. It was a few moments before he realised what had happened. He was no longer in the car but lying on the pavement. He sat up in a panic, patted himself down checking for injuries. His old jacket was unmarked, no scuffs on his elbow pads, no holes in the knees of his trousers. He felt his head and looked at his hands to see if there was any blood. His hands were clean. Having heard numerous stories of hip injuries in recent years he was relieved not to feel any pains in his bones or joints. It was a one in a million escape, he was completely injury free.

Joe stood up joyfully laughing, and looked around to see what was happening. His car was on its side, with its tail against the scrapyard wall. It did not take a doctorate in physics to realise which side of the car had been struck. Both side doors facing the sky had been smashed in. The body of the car was bent from the impact on the corner of the truck, it was resting on the side of the front half.

The jubilation evaporated when Joe saw a red smear was spread along the pavement and disappeared under the car. Passers-by stopped and held their breaths as they looked into the car, whilst others on the far side of the car were looking down at something else, with equal looks of horror on their faces. Some were hold-ing their hands to their mouths. Others turned away from the accident, freely vomiting into the gutters or bins, or just onto the pavement. Some were not so squeamish and appeared to be absorbing every detail. Others went further.

"What happened?" asked Joe.

Only a few people from the crowd looked up. A roughly dressed man, wearing a floppy black hat, that looked like some leather crudely shaped to fit on his head, with a dark scraggly beard and moustache and wide open eyes, popped his head up quickly. "Isn't it obvious?" he asked, before immediately returning his gaze to the accident, and feverishly drawing on a large white sheet of paper, on top of a pile of papers he was holding. His jacket was sleeveless and made of dark fur, like his tunic. His shoes looked like thick pieces of leather he had stood on, and then wrapped around his feet and roughly tied the sides together. He reminded Joe of a caveman.

"They don't care man," said a voice from behind, in a deep Caribbean accent. It resonated with warmth and reassurance. Joe span around to see a man with long black dreadlocks, cascading over the shoulders of an immaculate suit in green tweed, and neatly trimmed beard, wearing a matching wide brimmed hat, a red striped open collared shirt under his waistcoat, no tie, and brown polished leather shoes. He was holding a large reefer and waving it around as he spoke. Through puffy and stoned eyes, he looked directly into Joe's. Next to him was an Asian who appeared to be from the Indian subcontinent, wearing a sharp dark suit, a white shirt open at the collar and a loosened crimson coloured tie, with black polished shoes.

"Well, some o' them might," said the Rastafarian, laughing gently.

"Who are you?" asked Joe. "What do you mean they don't care?"

"We're the welcoming committee friend, and you're dead," said the Indian. "I'm Dan and this is Dude." He spoke in a deep accent like he was from the southern states of the USA. His smile was wide and sharp at the edges, with clean white teeth.

Joe was taken back by the bluntness of the dark suited man. He turned and looked more closely at the people scrambling around the mangled car. He looked at the mess that was the front of the truck, and the sight of the truck driver staring in shock at the wreckage.

"Welcoming committee?" asked Joe. The world was starting to spin, he reached out to grab something and steady himself. Dude took his arm and supported him with a firm grip.

"Damn it, man! Stop tellin' 'em we're the welcoming committee," said Dude. Dan merely smiled.

"Find Lilly man," said Dude. "I take care o' Joe."

The Indian flicked two fingers from above his eyebrow, in a mock salute, and wandered off. Dude attempted to help Joe to the ground and sit him at the edge of the pavement. Joe pulled his arm away. "I can get down myself," he said, lowering himself to the pavement. "I'm not decrepit! Who are you, anyway?"

"Like the man said, my name is Dude," was the reply.

"Dude? Really?" Joe was incredulous. "Is this some sort of hippy nonsense?" Then a thought occurred to him, 'Maybe I'm unconscious and this is all some sort of dream?'

Dude shrugged his shoulders. "Hippy nonsense? I look like a hippy?" He sighed. "Dude be my given name. Given t' me long ago, long before the ages o' man," he said. He took a draw on his reefer and slowly let out the smoke.

"Should you really be doing that?" asked Joe, looking at the Joint.

"Why not?" said Dude, "does it bother you?"

"Yes, it bothers me!"

"Chill man, your death is just the beginning. Y' gonna discover a lot o' new things."

Angrily Joe stood up. "This is nonsense!" he said, facing Dude. "This can't be real."

Dude sighed like a man who had seen it all before and slowly stood up.

"I must be fantasizing," said Joe. He scratched the top of his head.

Joe marched over to the people gathered around the car. There were sirens in the distance coming closer. "Hey," he shouted. "I'm right here."

The excited caveman popped up his head. "Oh, it's you again," he said. A few others looked in Joe's direction. Some were too distracted to look. A couple were glaring at the carnage and writhing pressed tight against each other, their hands wandering over their excited bodies. Joe was flabbergasted by their amorous behaviour, and then noticed more.

"Oh my god," gasped Joe. His eyes widened when he noticed the people who were rolling on the pavement in the blood.

Joe turned to look at Dude. "What the hell is going on? There's a couple making love in the blood," he said, pointing.

Dude took a draw on his joint. "Yes man, there's some that go that way." Dude put his arm around Joe's shoulders and turned him away from the carnage. "Y' know Jonah, y' got t' take it slow, just breath man, and feel the clean air inside," he said.

Dude was about to say more when Joe waved his hands in the air and turned to be face to face with Dude. "What the hell is your game!" demanded Joe. "Is this some kind of con?"

Dude was visibly surprised at the suggestion of a con, but he remained calm and his voice remained smooth like velvet, "No man," he said. "What kind o' con would I be playin', tellin' y' you're dead?"

Confounded by the question, "I don't know?" said Joe.

Dude put both of his hands on Joe's shoulders. They were big hands and yet gentle and soft as they soothingly caressed Joe's tense muscles. Looking directly into Joe's eyes he said softly, "You are dead, man."

"Then why does he see me? And them?" asked Joe, pointing at the stranger and those around him. "And why are those people having sex in public?"

"That's Ghan man. He's got some weird fetish man." Dude waved a hand in Ghan's general direction. "They all dead too."

Frustrated, Joe strutted up to the car to look inside and paused as soon as he could see the body pushed and crushed from the impact with the truck. He could still make out his face. the lifeless eyes still open and staring into space. The jaw absently shoved to the side. Hands, and arms strangely broken and twisted. Then through the windows he could make out parts of a woman's smashed body.

Joe stepped back. "Oh god!" he exclaimed. He swallowed and rubbed the back of his neck.

"I love that look on your face," said Ghan, some of those with him nodded and chuckled in agreement. "With your arms crossing like that, looks like you were having a fit."

"Shut up man," said Dude. "Y' know what I got t' do here. You're not makin' it easy."

"Dude, look at the way the car caught the woman, and drove her body across the pavement. You don't get that kind of spread often." He stepped back, laughing. "Look at that, her blood's spreading, and his is starting to flow a little more. Be a while yet before it hardens up." He went back to his sketching. Ghan's hands moved rapidly, and with precision, capturing the details without having to rub anything out.

Another bystander piped up and said to Joe, "That was a great hit. That truck just smashed into you and threw you off the road and you hit the kerb and twisted and flattened that woman and just slid across the pavement and, wow!"

Joe was appalled. Dude once again put a comforting arm around him and waved away the spectators. "Come back here man," said Dude guiding Joe back to the kerb, and sitting down again. Joe looked at the tarmac under his feet.

"Listen, try something for me man," said Dude. Joe looked at Dude sceptically. "Please man, it's a simple thing," said Dude.

Joe shrugged and said, "Why not?"

Dude smiled. "Now just close your eyes and breath deep."

"That's it?" asked Joe.

"That's it man."

So Joe closed his eyes, and took in a deep breath, slowly. He immediately opened his eyes in surprise. He noticed and separated the range of smells that surrounded him. The cars on the road, mixed with the scents of the Cherry blossom from the trees along the road, to the smell of the tarmac and the blood on the pavement. There was the aroma of an exotic fragrance from Dude. Then there was the smell of sweat and Joe turned to see a man wearing a tracksuit run around a corner straight into a man dressed like Dude's friend Dan, in a sharp dark suit with a red tie, the collar closed and tie pulled up, and shiny black shoes. The smartly dressed man didn't flinch as the running stranger bounced off him onto the ground. A woman in a casual but stylish dress and Cuban heels, appeared a moment later, running up to the fallen man. She stopped and looked over noticing Dude.

"Hey Dude," she said. "How's it going?"

"Different every time," said Dude. "Y' havin' trouble, Bee?"

Bee smiled sarcastically and said, "No," and went over to the fallen man. She helped him to his feet, and put her hands on her hips. "Please don't run again," she said. "I really don't need the exercise."

The stranger looked at the sharply dressed man who had stopped him in his tracks. "He moves fast for a big guy," he said. "How did he get here so quick?"

"Same way I should have," said Bee. "Look, just come with us, and we'll get you processed and settled."

"But I can't be dead," said the runner.

"I know," said Bee, sympathetically. "But it happened. You're died."

"But look at me," said the runner. "I keep fit, I eat right. Don't drink too much. What about my kids, and my wife?"

"I'm sure that insurance policy you took out will soften the blow for her," said Bee's friend. "Your wife was wise to encourage you to take the policy."

"But a stroke," said the runner. "I mean that's just not right. I only just turned fifty." Bee put her hand on his shoulder sympathetically and led him away.

"And she can spend more time with her boyfriend," continued the dark suited man.

Bee glared at her colleague who smiled at her wickedly. The runner looked horrified. "This way," said Bee, leading him away, walking a little faster. She sneakily punched the big man in the ribs. He flinched with the strike from the diminutive Bee, and distanced himself from her as they walked.

Joe, turning back to Dude, asked, "Why is my sense of smell so much stronger?"

"Not stronger man. You're just more aware of it. Your world just got bigger, man. Y' know y'ain't wearin' glasses?"

Joe's hands reached for his face. It was true, his glasses were gone and he could see clearly. The sky was crystal clear, a rich blue. The sun was still half way to its meridian. He could feel its warmth on his face. He put his hand to the ground and felt the rough texture of the paving stones and the smoother finish of the kerbstone.

"So this is it?" asked Joe. "It's all over?"

"Yah man. Your life here be done."

Joe sighed. "This can't be right."

Dude sat down next to Joe, and took another pull on his reefer. "Y' know Joe, y' can't predict what the future's got for y'. Reality's a complicated thing, 'n' it's not for us t' understand it all. Would y' guess that a wasp was the reason for y' crashin'? Mmm mm, Jah man. It's a crazy thing."

"A wasp? Is that what I felt? A wasp sting?"

Dude nodded. "Y' don't shut the window right man. Y' leave a little gap 'n' in it goes, tired. 'n' it was restin' nice till y' come 'n' sit your arse down on it."

"I don't believe it." Joe put his face into his hands,

just as he was struck on the shoulder. It was not a hard blow, but rather a sharp slap. Bringing his arms up to protect himself he turned to see a slender woman with long, wavey white hair glaring at him.

"Son of a bitch!" she shouted. "You killed me! Motherfucker!" This time she swung a small handbag at him.

Dan was behind her laughing. "Now now, Lilly," he said. "Be careful."

"Fuck you!" she snapped back confronting Dan, which only made his smile wider.

"You can say what you like, but you can't be doing harm to him, or anyone else. I'll let it go on this occasion, given the circumstances," he smiled amiably, through the obvious threat.

Instinctively Lilly shot back, "Or what!" with just the right amount of derision.

Dan had a look of relish in his eyes. Lilly was suddenly fearful, stepping back unable to keep Dan's gaze. Dude was quickly on his feet speaking in gentle tones. He stood in front of Dan, and said, "Now Dan man, the poor lady just died y' know. Y' see her make up, and the way she's set her hair? So fine, 'n' so elegant." He looked at Lilly. "The lady's wearin' her favourite blouse, with the frilly little sleeves. Y' think she make this effort for work?" Lilly looked Dude in the eye, and her own eyes softened. "No man, she was on the way t' see her grandson. She was going t' be with him all day. Can y' feel man?" Tears came up in Lilly's eyes. Dude continued in a gentle comforting voice, "She was gonna be with him all day, so her baby girl could be with her man. She was gonna give her a break. Finally, she was doing somethin' meaningful for her girl." Lilly began to cry, and Dude opened his arms and she took his embrace. Softly Dude said, "She got so many plans for the day man. Whatever he wants, she was ready. And life's been cruel t' the lady."

Dude let go of Lilly and turned to Dan, he put his hand on Dan's shoulder and passed him the Joint saying, "Now take a little o' this man." Dan took the Joint and sucked the smoke in deep. "Chill," continued Dude, "'n' find a little generosity in that black heart."

"Alright, alright," said Dan breathing out. "You can let go of my shoulder now. Go on, get back t' your business."

Dude turned back to Lilly. "Y' know, it's not his fault," said Dude, pointing at Joe. "Y' can't see an accident coming. Y' think he want t' crash 'n' die?"

Lilly looked away, she had taken out her handkerchief and was wiping her tears. "It was going to be such a special day. I've wanted it for so long."

"Ain't no right or wrong here, dear lady," said Dude.

"So what does this mean?" she asked. "What do we do?"

Dude laughed. "Y' can do a lot o' things." He threw his arms wide. "Whole o' creation out there waitin' t' be found. But we got t' get y' settled." He reached out and gently wiped away a tear.

Joe stood up. The guilt he felt was inescapable,

even though a part of him suspected none of this was real. "I'm sorry," he said to Lilly.

Lilly looked at Joe, and Joe saw more sadness than anger in her face. "Fuck you," she said.

Joe winced. Then he told himself, 'It's not real.' With a mental shrug, he half smiled and turned to Dude. "So what now?" he asked.

"Like I said t' the lady, time t' get y' settled, it's time for processing," said Dude.

"Of course," said Joe. "And what's processing."

"Bureaucracy, man," said Dude, chuckling. "The necessary. Come it takes no time at all."

"Ok," shrugged Joe. "Please lead on."

Dan paused and scrutinized Joe. "Now Jonah, is that cynicism I'm sensing from you?"

Joe looked around, and becoming agitated he said, "This does not meet with expectations. I am apparently dead, having accidentally killed this lady, and the Welcome to the Afterlife Committee is a dope smoking Rastafarian and an Asian in a very sharp black suit, with a generous hint of menace about him."

"And your point being?" said Dan. Joe's frustration seemed to enliven him.

Joe replied, "Aliens would have been more convincing. This is obviously a fantasy. I am caught in a dream of my own making. Maybe I did crash, but I'm not really dead, instead I'm in a coma."

"And your mind created us? And all o' this around you?"

"Of course." Joe looked around and for the first time noticed there were people in a variety of dresses, through the ages. There were also people in the sky, floating freely through the air. Then he noticed the people floating outside windows.

"Hey," said Lilly. "I am not a figment of your fucking imagination."

Dan turned to Dude. "Did you do the breathing thing?"

"Yeah man."

"Hmm. What about showing him the mess over there?" Dan pointed at the wreckage of Joe's car.

Joe was annoyed. "This is ridiculous!' he said. "Just take me to processing. Whatever that is."

Dude and Dan shrugged and Dan said, smiling, "Well alright, just follow us."

Looking back at the accident before they left, they saw Ghan was still drawing, and the strange people reveling in the gore and violence. There were others just looking out of curiosity. A policeman had arrived and he had moved people back, except those he could not see. "You know, your car really made one big mess of me," said Lilly. "Good thing I had my purse with my ID in it."

"Ghan was right," said Dan. "Once they move that car, Lilly's gonna take a mighty long time to clean up."

Sirens could be heard as the emergency services arrived. "Come, let's go," said Dude. They started walking down the pavement away from the accident.

Many people walked as if Dude's group wasn't there, others moved to make way. Dude turned to Dan, "Y' know that's for sharing man," he said. Dan smiled and returned the reefer to Dude.

As they walked Joe trailed behind, in his own thoughts, when a wasp flew by his head. He waved his hand to flick it away, but the wasp flew on as if oblivious of any attempt to swat it.

The pavement ran out as the streets and buildings disappeared. They were walking into the forest on a dry dirt track. There was a gentle breeze and the sky was still clear and bright. The air was crisp and Joe could make out the scents of the forest, in growing detail. Overhead he heard the birds, and their calls became more varied the deeper they went. High in the distance he saw objects fly above the trees. He could hear movement from the undergrowth. Dan rolled another Joint as they walked.

"So, I'm wondering, are we going to heaven or hell?" asked Lilly.

"That's up to you," said Dan, lighting the joint. The smoke billowed from his mouth.

"Then I choose heaven," said Lilly laughing. She looked at the Joint. "Can I have some of that?" she asked.

"Of course," said Dan, holding a draw in as he spoke and passed the joint.

Lilly took a drag. Joe watched her to see her reaction. She stopped walking and her eyes rolled shut, as she held the reefer at shoulder height, and reached out to steady herself. Dan took her hand. There was a glint to his eye.

"Wow!" said Lilly. She opened her eyes, and a wide grin stretched across her face. "That is amazing," she said. "If weed was this good when I was alive, I would never have quit."

"Why'd you quit?" asked Dan, appearing genuinely perplexed. Lilly was surprised by his question, and for a moment didn't know what to say.

"Dan man," laughed Dude. "Why do y' want t' trouble the lady?"

"I'm just curious is all," said Dan.

"Hmm. Y' got a job t' do, so be doin' it right."

"Alright Rasta man. Don't be getting all worked up now."

"Don't be callin' me Rasta Man."

"Dress like that what else am I gonna call you?"

"You know better man."

Lilly was distracted by the exchange, and then her eyes widened with a possibility. "Ooh, I just had a thought," she said. "Will we get to meet our family and friends?"

"Can't be predictin' the future lady," said Dude. "There's lots o' comin's 'n' goin's, and there's plenty dead, y' know." Lilly looked away disappointed with the answer.

Joe turned to Dude curiously and asked, "So how did you know to be there when we died?"

"I know nothing till the moment come. The

possibilities are many," said Dude. "Imagine man, y' might've survived."

"So we might not meet the people we knew before? What about my mother and father?" asked Lilly.

Dude turned to look at her. "Your momma 'n' poppa got great love for y' Lilly, there ain't no doubtin' it, and when they die, they move on."

Lilly's thoughts turned inward.

"I'd like to meet my wife," said Joe. "If this is all real, I know she'll be here and she'll be pleased to see me."

"What are y' sayin'? Seeing your wife's gonna make it real?"

"Call it my litmus test," said Joe. "She would wait for me. Just as I would have waited for her."

"Wow," said Lilly, cynically. "Listen to the romantic."

"I hope your right, man," said Dude, seeing the certainty in Joe's face. He turned and glanced at Dan.

Dan looked at Joe and said, "Maybe you should try a little bit o' that joint."

Joe immediately raised his hands. "Oh no," he said. "I tried it when I was a student, and it really didn't do anything for me. Just made me cough a lot. Never understood what people saw in it after that."

Dude laughed. "That grass y' smoke in Jake's room? The boy that quit in the first year?" he asked.

Joe nodded. "How do you know that?"

"I know that wasn't weed. His dealer took it from his garden, dried and crushed up he sold it. He got burned in a deal y' know, and was desperate for the cash."

"Really?" said Joe. "But Jake seemed to enjoy it so much."

Dude just laughed. "Maybe tomorrow y' try the real thing man, or maybe next week." He took the Joint from Lilly. "But if y' be dreaming, first y' got t' decide what it's gonna do t' y'."

"You have no idea what you're missing," said Lilly. "Sure making this shitty day a little easier to take."

Both Joe and Lilly were startled when a naked young woman ran across in front of them, laughing and giggling, chased by a naked young man, oblivious to the group walking the path. They disappeared into the bushes. When Joe and Lilly turned back, they were surprised again when within the trees a door appeared, floating freely in the air. It was made of wood and had a wooden frame, and both were painted a plain white. The handle glistened in the light and looked like gold. They both walked around it, amazed at what they saw, instantly forgetting the naked couple. Dude and Dan watched them assess what they were looking at.

"Ooh you got the white door," laughed Dan. Joe and Lilly looked at him, nervous about what that might mean.

"Now," smiled Dude. "You go in there, 'n' I see you on the other side. 'n' trust," he glanced at Dan, "the colour don't matter."

Joe and Lilly looked at the door, floating a few inches above the ground. They walked around it again, and came back to the side where Dude and Dan were stood.

"The door is just hanging there," said Joe. "The other side is right here."

"Damn it! Just open the door and go in," said Dan.

Surprised by Dan's outburst, Joe responded, "Keep your hair on son. This is all new to me."

"This is your dream Joe, roll with it," said Dan.

Dude put his hand on Dan's shoulder. "Easy," he said. Dan stepped back.

Joe reached out and turned the handle, and instead of the forest he saw the backs of rows of white seats, on a chromed tubular metal frame. There were people through the door. Amazed, Lilly and Joe looked at Dude and Dan. Dan sighed, "Every time," and Dude, smiling, waved them to go through. They hesitantly stepped into the frame and the other side. The door shut behind them and when they turned it was gone.

Chapter 2

Joe was in a place that looked like an airport waiting area. The rows of seats ran in parallel, five deep, all facing pedestals with attendants stood by them. The rows of seats were in groups next to one another, and the groups were in clusters, and the clusters disappeared into the distance to the left and right. The only light was from the windows high up at the top of the walls.

In front of each cluster was a square pedestal with an attendant. The attendants were of both sexes of a variety of nationalities and they were generally dressed in everyday clothes, with no particular pattern to any of them that suggested a uniform.

There were large screens above the attendants, with ten-digit numbers sequentially rolling over on them. Plain white screens with the numbers in black. People were sat waiting in the seats and getting up as their number appeared and walking to the attendants who took the tickets, and then indicated the flat surface of the pedestals. Hands were placed on the surfaces, and then they walked past the attendants, behind whom were doors of the same type as the one Joe and Lilly had just passed through.

Joe turned and looked around, and saw the ticket dispenser on the wall that had just appeared behind him. He took a ticket and looked at it. The number was large and printed in print so small that Joe automatically squinted to read it, before realising he could read it easily despite its size. He pulled another one and offered it to Lilly.

"Well, this looks easy," said Joe.

"Yeah, whatever," said Lilly, ignoring Joe's offer of a ticket and took another for herself. She marched off and took a seat.

Joe went after her and sat down next to her.

"You know what?" said Lilly, angrily. "I'd prefer it if you'd sit somewhere else."

"Look I'm sorry," said Joe. "We had an accident. I didn't mean to kill you."

Lilly crossed her arms and sat stiff and upright looking forward. But Joe could see the way her nostrils flared and her chest rose and fell. "What the fuck do you care any way!" she said. "You think you're just dreaming."

She was right. Why did he care? If this was a dream then he could change it. He focused and thought of a better version of Lilly. She looked at Joe quizzically. "What the fuck are you doing?" she asked.

"What do you mean?" he asked.

"You look like you're constipated," she said.

"What are you talking about? I do not look like that."

"Yes, you do. Your jaw's all knotted up. Looks like your whole body's clenched up, and trying to squeeze out a big shit."

Joe turned away. "I was concentrating," he said.

Lilly laughed. "That your thinking face?"

"Yeah, I was hoping to think you away," said Joe.

Lilly laughed even more. "Dumbass."

After a moment to calm down, Joe sighed and said, "Well, clearly I have no control over my subconscious, like everyone else in the world."

"You're not dreaming arsehole. You're really dead, and you can't wish me away. And yes, you can change your dreams."

Joe turned away, feeling frustrated because Lilly was right, he should be able to put aside any responsibility towards her. This apparent death was a figment of his imagination. Yet he couldn't help but feel the weight of responsibility.

Whilst Joe attempted to restore a more peaceful frame of mind, a young man slouched into the seat next to him. His jeans, the hooded sweatshirt, and trainers were old, worn and torn. He was unkempt, with skin sallow, and Joe guessed he was homeless. He had a baffled expression on his face, and appeared anxious as he scanned the space around him. His right knee was twitching, and his heel rapidly went up and down.

"How are you doing?" asked Joe, in part to stop the vibrating knee.

The knee stopped. "I'm alright," said the young man sharply, sitting up. "Why?" he asked.

Joe raised his hands. "Whoa," he said. "Take it easy. I'm just as confused as you are."

"Yeah, sure," said the young man, he slouched back into his seat and the knee started to twitch again.

"So, what happened to you?" asked Joe.

The knee stopped again. The young man looked at Joe suspiciously.

"Oh come on. What does it matter? Apparently, we're dead. So, what's bothering you?" said Joe.

"Yeah, I guess," the young man conceded.

"What are you so nervous about?" continued Joe.

"What am I so nervous about?" the young man spoke fast, agitation returning to his voice. "Shit! I didn't exactly lead a good life man. I fucked up. Whatever's through that door can't be good." He looked at the door behind the attendants.

Joe paused for a moment. "Well maybe it's not as bad as you might think."

The young man turned to face Joe. "I'm dead cos I got shot robbing a house man! I'm hooked on smack. I fucking rob people to buy drugs. Really pissed off my family. They don't want to know me. I'm fucked man!"

Joe fidgeted in his seat. "I'm sorry to hear that," he said.

"Yeah, that's great. You look like you're going to the good place. After all the shit I've done, it's fire and brimstone for me. Fuck man!" His knee started to twitch more vigorously than before.

"It might not be," said Lilly. "You don't know for sure."

"I know lady. Once my hand goes on that thing they got up there, that's it! All the shit I've done's gonna come up and that door's gonna open to fucking hell."

"Oh, don't be like that," said Lilly. "Your life's over, yeah, but nothing's just black and white."

The young man sat back again. "Yeah, maybe you're right," he said. "Maybe it's just another life."

"There you go," smiled Lilly.

"Hey we can't all be going to different places," said Joe.

"Why not?" said Lilly, still expressing her anger at Joe.

Joe bit his tongue, though he couldn't keep the tension out of his voice. "Because we all go through the same door."

"Well maybe it's a magic fucking door, like the one that fucking brought us here?" rasped Lilly. Joe concluded that her anger had not waned.

"But it brought us all to the same place," replied Joe, in a smaller voice.

"Oh shit. I'm coming back as a fucking ant. Or a bug or something." The young man's head fell into his hands.

Lilly turned back to the young man. "Oh no," she said. "I mean it could be anything. Christ, you might come back as a lion."

The young man sniggered.

Joe asked. "Does any of this fit with what you were expecting when you died?"

"What? I don't know man. I look like I was fucking religious to you? What the fuck do you think?"

"Well, it's not what I expected," said Joe. "I wasn't sure there would be anything to look forward to. If there was an afterlife, I always thought there would be a moment of awakening, maybe I would have an epiphany, and I would gain a new understanding of the universe. Discover the purpose of my existence."

"No pearly gates, right?"

"Well. No, I suppose not," said Joe. "Though I'm a Jew."

The youth looked confused, and said, "Whatever." The foot started to twitch again, and the young man stared at the door.

Joe looked more intently at the door. "I suppose the door might be a pearl white colour," he said.

"Maybe there are no pearly gates man, but just a fucking door that takes you where you deserve to go."

"And you think you deserve to be punished?" said Joe.

"What the fuck do you think?"

"I don't know," said Joe. "But that's the point. This is nothing like I was expecting. There were people having sex on the pavement in the blood when I died."

The young man stopped twitching and looked at Joe skeptically.

"Yeah, that was fucking weird. That was my blood. Mostly," said Lilly.

"What the fuck are you talking about lady?"

"My blood was all over the pavement after this fucker killed me, and some people turned up to see what happened. And some of them started to roll around on the pavement, and messed around with each other. A couple were definitely having sex."

The youth stared at Lilly and Joe, and then burst out into a cackling, quickfire laugh.

"Never mind all that," said Joe, and asked, "So was it quick for you?"

The young man's face dropped. "What dying?"

Joe nodded.

"No man. I got shot and it took fucking forever to die man," said the youth, speaking quickfire. "I was like bleeding for fuck knows how long. Shit, I could feel the life slipping out o' me. Bitch that shot me was screaming and crying for forever before she called a fucking ambulance. I was screaming for so fucking long, trying to stop the blood from pouring out of me, and then I couldn't move or scream anymore." The youth paused, reflecting on the moment. "Funny, you don't know what you've done until it's too late. The whole fucking time I was thinking what the fuck did I do? All the shit I did was going through my head, and I even wondered if my folks would even come to my fucking funeral. Shit like that. Got to wonder. I mean I didn't do a fucking thing man. Nothing meaningful, you know. It all just kept running through my mind.

And all the time I wished I could have one more hit before I went. Thought that talk was bullshit, but fuck me did I want that hit! Then it all went dark. Then I was stood in front of me and I was looking at my dead body and the fucking woman was crying and there was Dude, and Dan."

Lilly screamed. "You met Dude too!"

"But that's not possible," said Joe. "We were just with him."

"You mean the Rasta with long dreads, and the very cool suit?"

"Yes!" shrieked Lilly. "Did you try his weed?"

The young man's eyes lit up. "Oh man," he said dreamily. "That Joint was like fucking kicking it out man!" They laughed together.

"But that's not possible," said Joe.

"Why not?" asked the young man.

"Yeah, Joe. Why not?" asked Lilly.

"Because we just left him," said Joe, exasperated. "We haven't been here that long."

"Maybe time works differently now," said Lilly.

Joe scoffed, "Time works differently?"

"Yeah," said the youth. "I mean shit, we shouldn't even be here. This is like magic or some shit man."

"That's right," said Lilly.

Joe laughed. "Like magic?" he said.

"Why the fuck not?" said Lilly.

Joe didn't respond. He looked away from Lilly.

"And there's that fucking door," said the young man. His knee started to twitch again.

"Aren't you meeting Dude on the other side?" asked Lilly. "He told us he would meet us on the other side."

"Yeah, told me that too. But where's he gonna take me?"

They all stared at the door.

An elderly man sat down next to Lilly, smiling to himself. "Hello," said Lilly.

The old man turned to Lilly. "Hello," he said cheerily.

"I'm guessing you died of natural causes," she said.

Still smiling he said, "If you call a heart attack natural causes."

"I wouldn't know. What were you doing when it happened?"

"I just finished doing the most natural thing of all. I had sex with a really hot young woman," grinned the old man. "She finished me off with the best blowjob I ever had."

After the initial surprise all three joined in the laughter with the old man, two of them nervously. "Vin sure came through this time," he said. "Worth every penny."

"Not what I was expecting," said Lilly.

"You don't say," said Joe.

"Old dog," laughed the young man. "Still got some mojo."

"You bet," smiled the old man. "That and a little blue pill." He laughed.

"What about the girl?" asked Lilly, "She must have been freaked."

"Not my first heart attack," smiled the old man.

"She was on her way out, when I felt it coming on. The goodbye kiss pushed me over the edge. The door slammed shut and I hit the floor. Smiling. From Cheek to cheek." He started laughing out loud. The others became caught up in his mirth.

"So how did you two die," asked the old man.

"Oh he hit me with his car," laughed Lilly.

"No shit," said the old man.

"It's not that simple," said Joe. "I was hit by a truck first."

"Only because you weren't paying attention," replied Lilly.

"But Lilly please," pleaded Joe. "I was stung by a wasp."

The young man's laugh was quick fire, and shot out as he curled up with a wide grin. "You know old man, I haven't laughed like this in fuckin' years. Fuckin' crazy how there's so many ways to die. Thought I'd go up in a blaze. ODed with no fuckin' idea the lights were out. Shit! I wish I'd gone like that."

They stopped laughing and they were sombre when Joe's number came up on one of the screens. Joe got up and went to the pedestal where the attendant took his number and then threw it over his shoulder. Joe looked at what she had done and the attendant indicated the pedestal. Joe put his hand on the stone and felt nothing. No sound was heard, nor was there a light or any other indication of anything happening. The attendant indicated the door. Joe looked back at Lilly, who got up and approached the pedestal, when her number appeared on the screen. Joe waited to see what would happen with Lilly. The same happened again, the attendant casually threw the number away and absolutely nothing happened when Lilly put her hand on the stone. They looked at the door and took a look at the two men who had sat with them. They both waved, the old man with his broad grin and jubilance, and the young man with a short wave of his hand. The youth's eyes on the door, and his knee twitching rapidly.

Joe went to the door and Lilly followed quickly behind him. He reached out and opened the door. He walked through and before the door shut Lilly followed him.

Chapter 3

The door closed behind Joe and Lilly and they were once again in the forest, where Dude and Dan were waiting for them. They were surrounded by the wafts of smoke from the cone they had been smoking.

Dude had a broad grin on his face. "They come on time. You fine, Joe 'n' Lilly?" he asked.

"Ok I guess," said Joe.

"Fine," said Lilly.

"There's a guy in there saying you met him just a few moments ago. But you were with us. How's that possible?" asked Joe.

Dude spread his hands and said, "Magic."

Dan chuckled. "Shit Joe, you don't even believe this is real. Just enjoy the ride."

Joe ground his teeth, and muttered, "Of course. Hmph."

"He's got a point y' know," said Dude indicating Dan. "Y' here, it's now, man. Feel what's around you."

Joe pursed his lips and looked around.

"Maybe he's in denial because he killed me," said Lilly.

"It was an accident!" said Joe.

"If this is all fake, I guess you didn't," said Lilly.

"Ja! The lady got a point too." Dude laughed.

Irritated Joe said. "Look is there anything else? Do I just wander off? Are you going to be with me while I wander through this fantasy?"

"Not all o' that man. Right now, I only got one thing for both o' you."

"What?"

"I got y' a place t' stay, man."

"What place?" asked Joe.

"A house, of course," said Dan. "Unless you want to sleep outside in the open." He sounded serious.

"A house?"

"Don't you want a house?" asked Dan.

"Well, yes, I suppose I'll need a place to stay," said Joe. "But I'm... I don't know what I am." He looked away, uncertain.

"Huh?" muttered Dude, confused by Joe's uncertainty.

"Well, when you know, be sure to let us know," said Dan. There might have been a roll of his eyes, but Joe didn't see it.

"Chill Dan," laughed Dude. "Come. Y' gonna love it man," he said to Joe.

Dude led the way, as they walked a worn path, and went up the side of a hill. The journey was occasionally interrupted by distant sounds of thunder, though there wasn't a cloud in the sky. Overhead Joe could see the shadow of large birds, and some things he was sure he was fantasizing, like a shoal of fish shooting past the tops of the trees, and from the bushes came a variety of sounds. On three occasions Joe saw bushes shaking, and heard what he thought were moans and groans.

Joe had no idea how long he had been walking, and when Dude stopped and announced they had arrived, Joe had no sense of place. What he had was a view from the foothills of a mountain, across a valley that was bright with light, and the many shades, and scents of the forest. It was warm and fresh. Nature was all about him, with all its potent vibrancy. Breathing in he felt the clean air. The breeze seemed to wash his face and as he breathed out, the tension that had been holding on to his shoulders slipped away.

Dude was indicating a small path between the trees. Joe did not ask any questions, he just walked towards the path. After a small distance the forest cleared to reveal a house with vistas across the valley, and the mountains.

Joe was stunned by the size of the building. He stood admiring its height and breadth. The main entrance was a large door of dark wood. There was a large brass knocker in the middle of it, and a wide letterbox. The building spread to the left and right, at an obtuse angle, meeting at the main entrance. Over the main door was a large window framed in the same dark wood.

"A little big just for me," said Joe.

"No man. Not just you. You both got this place," said Dude.

Joe and Lilly turned to Dude, "Are you fucking kidding?" said Lilly, her disbelief etched across her face.

"Like the man said, it's a big house. Too much for just one," said Dude.

"Yes, I know, but this is awkward," said Joe. "Look at her," They all looked at Lilly, whose expression could not be described as happy or excited at the prospect of sharing a house with Joe. "I don't want to live with her. She's so angry," said Joe.

"Mmm, so maybe your mind's trying t' teach y' something?"

"He wrecked my big day and I am pissed off! I do not want to share a house with this fucker!" said Lilly.

"You hear that?" said Joe. "You put me in there with her, there's no telling what she'll do to me."

Dude scoffed, "Psh, y' know there ain't any truth there. Your mind gonna kill y'?"

Joe looked at her glaring eyes, and flared nostrils. She held herself back behind gritted teeth. "I'm not so sure about that Dude," said Joe. "It's not like my normal dreams. I can't change a thing."

Dan sighed. "This house is for both o' you, but you're free to find somewhere else if you want. It's sure nice out here. The stars are spectacular."

"I'm not sleeping outside. I'm too old for that nonsense," said Joe.

"So, it's settled," said Dude.

Dan looked at Dude. "I think we're done here," he said quickly. "We're needed elsewhere."

"Doors open," said Dude.

With that Dude and Dan wandered up the path and back into the forest, the pungent odour of the weed trailing behind them.

"What?! NO!" shouted Lilly. "You can't just leave." She chased after them, as they walked through the trees. After a few moments she came back looking around seething with anger. "They just fucking disappeared!" she said.

Joe was rubbing his brow. He looked at the house and looked around. There was no obvious place to go. He hadn't paid attention to the route as they had arrived. The house was solitary with no other place in sight and no signs of life other than the wild creatures he could hear so clearly, and those that were flying in the sky.

"It's a big place," said Joe, "and we've got the whole forest out here. We don't ever have to see each other if we don't want to."

Lilly suddenly pushed past Joe towards the house, declaring, "I'm choosing my room first."

Joe watched Lilly march off to the house, and followed slowly. "I don't believe it," he muttered to himself. "I'm supposed to be in the afterlife and there's a housing shortage."

When Lilly opened the door, it got stuck immediately against something behind it. Joe would've helped her, but Lilly made it clear she did not need his help with a simple, "Fuck off!" When they got in, there were a pile of flyers behind the door. Joe pushed the high pile aside, and they looked around.

The house was beautiful. Just what Joe and his wife had talked about all those years ago, when they had made plans as a young couple. A beautiful spacious hallway with wide stairs either side leading up to the landing, with carved wooden bannisters, and high windows all round. All following the Art-Deco style of design. A style, he discovered, that was followed throughout the house.

There were two hallways following the angle of the two sides of the house. The wide balcony was in three sections. One either side from the stairs in front of the two corridors and the third joining the other two together.

Lilly appeared on the left side balcony. "I've got my room, you're in the one furthest away from mine!" she shouted down, then swiftly turned and went back to her room.

"I didn't know you were picking my room as well," muttered Joe. "Hope it's got a good lock." He went to investigate the ground floor rooms. The window above the door was the main source of light for the hallway, apart from the large chandelier, which wasn't on. Joe chose the corridor that was immediately to his left, going under the section of balcony Lilly had appeared on.

There was a door to a washroom, which boasted a large space with a sink and mirror, and everything for those necessary touches a person might need before going out. Another door led to a large cloakroom, where there were rails and hangars on two sides, with a shoe rack under each of the rails, stacked three high and filled with shoes, men's and women's, of various sizes and styles, with a variety of coats on the rails.

At the end of the corridor were three doors, one to either side and a third on the end wall. Joe went through the door to his left, into the kitchen. The kitchen was on the front side of the house. He looked around at the equipment, and all that he would have wanted was there. There was ample space for the extended island. The design of the cabinets and equipment followed through from the rest of the house. The large fridge was filled with fresh food and drink. He thought it was odd that there was food in the afterlife, but then again, he was in a house in a forest in the afterlife.

A window stretched across one wall and revealed views of the forest, and at the end past a large breakfast table, was a door leading to a fully equipped utility room. The side of the breakfast area was open, and led into the dining room. The dining room opened into a wide and long room, with enough space to include tables with two chairs by each, along the windows. On the opposite wall were cabinets for the cutlery and other table furniture. In the middle of them was the door leading to the hall. The dining table and other furniture was made of wood with a light-coloured grain, and the tables were inlaid with beautiful images of wildlife and fruit and vegetables. The dining table was decorated with three candelabras evenly spaced along its length.

At the far end of the room there was an open section of wall, to match the one from the kitchen.

"Magnificent," muttered Joe, when he entered the living room.

The outside wall of the living room was all glass, from the floor to the ceiling. The height of the ceiling was more than another floor above, and Joe estimated at least twice as wide. It revealed a view across the valley to the mountains on the far side.

A section of the glass showed sliding doors allowing access to the large patio area at the back, with garden furniture already set out. Beyond the patio the land was clear and sloped gently into the forest, and connected to trails running into it. To the side Joe could see the other part of the house with a long wall and high windows running along it. It disappeared into the trees and Joe wondered what could be in it.

Three long leather sofas were placed to make the three sides of a square, with the glass wall as the fourth side. In the centre was a large square coffee table, with drawers on all sides. The sofas were only one part of the room, the next part had occasional oval tables, beautifully finished to maintain the design style. Then another section had seating for individuals and groups. Coffee tables, and other furniture were placed around the room. There were cupboards, but the wall at the end rose high above them, and was completely blank. Thinking about the shape of the building, with the wide angle between the two sides, there was a space in the middle that must have been taken up in some way.

The furniture was extensive, but there was not a single picture on the walls or plants anywhere in the house. The walls were all painted a neutral colour. Any decorations and furniture followed the same unassuming palette.

Joe dropped into the sofa facing the giant window wall and looked at the world outside. He remembered the truck and it hitting the car. Then he remembered waking up on the pavement. 'Nonsense!' he thought. 'I would've woken up in the car if I'd died in it." Cabinets to the side held glasses and he was sure there would be drinks in them as well. When he looked there were a variety of wines and spirits to choose from. The number and quantity of alcoholic drinks was more than he would drink in a year. He picked a bottle of wine that was a screw top, and poured himself a glass and returned to his seat.

Joe was lost in a train of thought when he was surprised by Lilly suddenly speaking from behind him. "Wow, what a view," she said.

"It is beautiful," he replied.

"You've got wine," she said, pleased. She looked around, saw the cabinet and went and got a glass. "Pour me some," she said, putting the glass on the coffee table. Joe looked up at her and considered for a moment, before pouring the wine. As Joe poured, she sat down at the other end of the sofa to take in the view.

"Oh! My! God!" she said, after taking a sip of the wine. "That is fucking good wine."

Joe smiled. "I felt the same when I got my first taste," he said, raising his glass.

"Mind you, I haven't had a drink in years, so any wine is going to taste fucking amazing." She downed the glass and poured herself more wine.

"Here's to death," she continued, taking another mouthful. Sitting back, "This house is fucking amazing," she said.

"Yes it is," said Joe.

Though Lilly's mood appeared to have changed, he could still hear the anger underlying everything she said. "It's the kind of place my wife and I always wanted."

"Yeah, me too," said Lilly, thoughtfully. "Is there any music? I always wanted the ultimate sound system. We need to liven things up around here."

Joe pointed to a cabinet to the side of the drinks cabinet. "There's stereo equipment in there," he said.

Lilly lifted herself out of the seat and opened the cabinet and found a single unit, with a screen at the top. She stared at it for a moment and then touched it, and a few seconds later was heard to say, "Cool."

Rich clear music emanated from hidden speakers. Lilly stood back smiling, as the smooth jazz filled the room.

"You don't seem so angry now," said Joe.

"Yeah, what am I going to do? Looks like I'm dead, for whatever fucking reason, so I'll deal with it the best way I can. And anyway, the big plus is that I have this great house, with wardrobes full of clothes, with names on labels I've never heard of, but they are fucking amazing, make up and God knows what else. It's like I hit the fucking lottery jackpot after a year of fucking rollovers. The only thing wrong is it comes with a Joe."

"Yes," muttered Joe. "Make the most of it."

"Damn right I'll make the most of it."

Lilly continued to look around the room, and then she whooped at a discovery. "I found shot glasses," she announced. "And I know where the tequila is."

Lilly returned to a second sofa, square to Joe's. She put the tequila and shot glasses on the coffee table. "Now for the lime and salt," she said. She skipped off to the kitchen and returned with the final ingredients.

Cheerfully Lilly loaded a line of shot glasses, with a saucer of slices of lime, and a salt cellar to the side. She put a small amount of salt on her hand by the thumb, licked it, downed a shot and sucked on a slice of lime. "Shit that's good," she said. She then took her glass of wine.

Joe quietly sipped on his wine. Lilly looked at him and asked. "Why the fuck did they stick us together?" she asked.

"Did you miss the bit about not enough houses?" said Joe.

"Yeah right," said Lilly. She took down the next shot.

"I've only seen this part of the house, and there's that other big corridor, and you won't believe what's upstairs."

"The house has everything you could want," muttered Joe, thoughtfully.

Lilly considered Joe for a moment. "You know what you need?"

"What?"

Lilly pointed at her line of tequilas. "You need a shot."

"Are you out of your mind," objected Joe. "I haven't done that sort of thing in decades."

Lilly laughed. "Seriously?" she asked. "Shit, you need this more than me." Joe pursed his lips, indignantly. "Oh come on," she said. "What the fuck can it hurt? I gave up booze and all the drugs so I could rebuild a relationship with my daughter and her family. Took me a long fucking time and your..." she searched for the word, "negligence cost me everything. So, you're going to fucking join me in having a fucking shot of tequila."

Joe looked angrily at Lilly, he could not hold her gaze however. She had all the fury of the wronged and he raised his hands in submission. "Alright, alright," he said, and reached out to pick up one of the glasses. "You know you really don't need to swear so much."

"Fuck off," said Lilly. Then seeing Joe reaching for

the shot glass said, "Hold on. You've got to get the salt and the lime ready."

"I've done Tequila shots before!" said Joe.

"Alright, alright," said Lilly. "Keep your fucking hair on."

"Ha, ha!"

Joe arranged the salt and the lime, whilst Lilly watched closely as Joe licked the salt, quickly tipped the tequila into his mouth, and sucked on the lime. His face was squashed into a pile of wrinkles as the intense tang of the lime washed away the last of the salt and mixed with the flavour of the Tequila. Then Joe realized he could taste the drink. He could make out each of the ingredients as they mixed in his mouth. The liquid was not hard, as he remembered it, as it made its way down his throat. It sat softly in his stomach. He remembered doing the shots in his youth, before those times petered away over the years.

Lilly threw her arms in the air. "That's how you do it!" she cheered. "Halle-fucking-lujah!"

As the day rolled on, Lilly gave up on the Tequilas and settled into the wine. Another and then another bottle was drunk, and at some point in the early evening they found themselves on the patio, watching the daylight fade and the brilliance of the stars grow. The stars were so numerous that both Lilly and Joe were overwhelmed by the wonder before them.

Occasionally Joe could see points of light in the distance, appearing to rise up into the sky.

"Amazing," whispered Joe. "Totally amazing."

"Well, hey," said Lilly. "This needs a little something more." She reached into her back pocket and took out a reefer.

"Where did you get that?" asked Joe.

"Dan made it for me on the way here." She smiled wickedly. "Want some?" she asked.

"Oh, I don't know," said Joe.

"Come on!" she said. "Live a little."

Joe laughed. "'Live a little'," he muttered. "Yeah sure, why not? What the hell, I'm supposed to be dead. What have I got to lose?"

"That's the spirit," said Lilly. Joe laughed again. "But first I need a light." She looked around, and saw nothing useful.

"There are drawers in the coffee table," said Joe. "Maybe there's something in one of them."

Lilly went back to the coffee table and returned smiling. "I guess they think of everything," she said.

"Whoever they are," said Joe. He sat up as Lilly lit the joint, and watched her suck in the smoke. She held the smoke in her chest whilst passing the reefer to Joe. Joe took the joint tentatively and sucked on the end. Lilly breathed out saying, "Wow that is smooth." Joe expected his lungs to react and force him into a fit of violent coughing, just as he'd seen his friends do when they'd smoked a cigarette as kids. Seeing them cough and wretch had convinced Joe not to try it himself. This time nothing happened. It was a short pull, and his lungs were fine.

"Don't be a pussy," said Lilly through the vapour falling out of her mouth and floating around her face. "Take a lung full."

Joe shrugged his shoulders, and took a long, deep drag. He leaned back, and stared up at the sky as he let the smoke out slowly. It didn't burn or make him cough, instead he felt a gentle rush wash up his back and a lightness come over him. Soon they were both lying on their backs looking up at the stars, listening to the sounds of the forest, and the music coming out of the house through the open glass doors. There were so many sounds, that Joe wondered why he could hear so much. His nose was already working overtime.

"This is the best," said Lilly. "When I was alive it was never like this." She pointed up at the sky. "Look at all those stars," she said. "Aren't they beautiful?"

"The light pollution in the city would have hampered your view of the stars. I saw something like this when I was at the observatories in the mountains. But this is better."

"It's all better," said Lilly. "The wine, the smoke, the sky. I really must be in heaven. Apart from being stuck with you."

"It's not real," said Joe.

Lilly turned to look at him. "What? Do you still think you're dreaming?" she asked.

"It's all just part of my imagination," he said. "My subconscious finding ways to comfort me."

Lilly rolled her eyes, and sat up. "Hey listen pal,"

she said. "I'm not part of anybody's fucking imagination. Maybe you're part of mine, how about that?"

Joe continued to look up at the stars. Smiling he said, "Maybe I am."

"But Joe, the sounds and smells. For fuck's sake, the way this all feels when I touch it," Lilly ran her fingers along the surface of the stone on which she sat. "I've never had a dream that felt like this."

"No," agreed Joe.

"You need to stop that crazy talk, and get your fucking head straight," said Lilly. She then started to carefully stand up. "I'm going to get more booze." Precariously she walked to the house, in anything but a straight line. A few minutes later she staggered out with a fresh bottle of wine. She dropped to the ground and sat cross-legged. For a moment she stared at the bottle. "Shit! It's corked. I thought they were screw tops," she said.

"There are plenty of screw tops," said Joe. "If you'd looked."

"Good to know. Where's the fucking corkscrew?" she asked.

"In the cabinet."

"Shit!" she said and got up, precariously.

When Lilly returned, she had the corkscrew and a bowl of fruit. "You hungry?" she asked.

"No," said Joe, "But I'll eat."

Before the bottle was opened several of the fruit were eaten. As like the other food and drink the fruit was delicious. Better than any he had had before. Joe lay back down, whilst Lilly returned to the task of opening the bottle. Eventually she served the drinks and lay back. She looked at the stars for a moment and then sat back up.

"Alright," she said. "Say I go along with you. Why the fuck would your subconscious make me, the person you kill in a car accident? And why the fuck would I end up sharing a house with you in the afterlife? Why would it even create a situation where you're told you're dead?"

"I don't know," said Joe. "I'm a physicist, not a psychologist."

"Pssh," spluttered Lilly.

"You know we talked about this already?"

"I'm fucking wasted so expect a little repetition."

After a moment as Lilly silently drank her wine, and rocked back and forth, Joe said, "What about the processing? The two guys one old, one young. Didn't that seem a little contrived to you?"

"Coincidence," said Lilly.

"Possibly."

"Hey anything's possible. That's what the scientists keep telling us."

"Yes, but..."

"But nothing. I am not a figment of your goddamn imagination. Shit would your imagination have ever come up with Dude? And Dan?"

"No," said Joe. "They're nothing like I would've expected. I mean they smoke so much cannabis."

"There you go." She reached for the reefer and

then looked around. "Damn it! I left the lighter in the house." She got up precariously, and wobbled her way into the living room.

Joe lay back down and looked up at the stars.

"And another thing." Lilly had got back and was waving the lighter in Joe's general direction. "Why would your subconscious let you think you were dead if you're not?"

"You already asked me that," laughed Joe.

"I did?" she dropped down to the floor. "God I am so fucking wasted." She lit the Joint.

"Me too," said Joe.

"You don't look it, and you don't sound it."

"Just because I'm not slurring my speech doesn't mean I'm not wasted. You wait till I try to get up."

Lilly giggled. "I'll wait to see that," she said. She lit the joint and took several more draws and blew the smoke at Joe, before passing it. Joe refused the joint, his head was spinning and he found himself on the verge of talking gibberish. Lilly put her legs out and lay down. "What a wonderful view. It's so ... humbling," she said.

There was a flash among the trees in the distance, and then the sound of an explosion, loud, and rumbling and the crack of lighting. As they watched the stars, barely reacting to the flash and the thunder, a point flared through the sky above, like a meteor, trailing a line of smoke behind it. Joe tried to look more closely and thought he discerned a slender figure, with flailing arms and legs, ablaze as they flew through the air.

"What was that?" asked Joe.

"Comet?" guessed Lilly. The conversation did not go much further and silently they passed out.

Chapter 4

Joe's face was wet, and his nose was filled with the powerful scent of what he thought was a dog. He opened his eyes and shook his head. He jumped up onto his feet when he saw the wolf. The wolf looked at him inquisitively, a creature with luscious white fur and piercing grey eyes. There was no threat from it, none the less Joe was scared. His gaze fixed on the wild animal, he staggered backwards away from the wolf and fell over Lilly. Shocked into wakefulness she quickly sat up with a clenched fist, holding the left-overs of a joint between her top two fingers, shouting, "What the hell's going on?"

Joe pointed at the wolf. Lilly looked at the wolf and immediately froze. "Oh," she uttered.

The wolf approached Lilly, sniffing inquisitively before licking her clenched hands.

"Hey watch the joint," said Lilly, pulling her hand away.

The wolf appeared to be listening to what Lilly was saying. She reached out her other hand, and the wolf sniffed it and moved up so her hand was against the fur on its neck.

"Oh, it's friendly," said Lilly, relaxing and then starting to stroke the creature.

Joe stared in disbelief whilst Lilly readily dropped her guard and allowed a creature that could rip out her throat in an instant, nuzzle around her neck as she giggled with delight. He looked around and noticed there were many other wolves. There was an entire pack around them. In a hushed voice Joe said, "They're in the house."

The wolf that had licked Joe's face sat down next to Lilly. "Oh, he is the sweetest thing," she said, stroking his fur.

Others of the pack came and sat around with the two humans. Joe closed his eyes and tried to calm himself. When he opened his eyes, the wolves were still there, and comfortably sat taking in the view. One then walked up to Joe and tried to lick his hand. Joe stiffened up pulling his hands back close to his chest, breathing sharply.

"Stroke it," said Lilly. "Their fur is so soft."

"I have to admit, I'm still a little nervous," said Joe looking around as if to find an escape route.

"Hey it's your dream," said Lilly. "Chill out."

"I might be wrong. This could be a nightmare?" said Joe.

Despite his reluctance Joe did not sense any form of aggression from the wolves, if anything he felt they were just curious. He reached out his hand and started to stroke the wolf next to him. It welcomed his touch. Its fur was soft and comforting.

Within a few minutes there was a transformation and several of the wolves were being petted by Joe. Joe and Lilly stood up and began to play with them. After a while they sat back down and the wolves sat down around them. Joe felt relaxed, the animals seemed to have the power to make him forget his stresses.

"Are you hungry?" asked Joe.

"No," said Lilly. "Are you?"

"No."

"Are you hung over?"

Joe thought for a moment. "No," he said, curious. "But I should be. We put away a lot of wine. Not to mention the shots. I tell you what I would like."

"What?"

"Coffee."

"Oh yeah."

They got to the kitchen and looked at the coffee machine. The wolves followed Joe and Lilly into the house and sniffed around the room and furniture. They watched Joe work out the coffee machine, whilst Lilly went to the fridge and investigated its contents. She gasped, "There's so much food," she said. She then looked in the cupboards and found more food and ingredients. She took out a packet of biscuits and offered some to the wolves. They looked at the offering with interest, before one tasted a biscuit and decided it liked it and the others came to her sniffing for the rest. Smiling, Lilly put a biscuit in her mouth and started to pass them out to the wolves. All the biscuits were soon gone, and the wolves looked at her again as if asking a question. In answer she showed them the empty packet. The wolves sat on their haunches and looked disappointed. Lilly opened another packet.

The aroma of fresh ground coffee beans tantalizingly wafted across the kitchen. As the machine poured the dark liquid into the cups, Joe's anticipation rose. He turned around with two cups of coffee, and noticed Lilly finishing her biscuit and the empty packet. "You ate all of them?" he asked incredulously.

"I got one," she said taking a cup from Joe. "The wolves got yours."

Joe was irked, but his curiosity was peaked and he asked, "How was it?"

"I could lie, but you know it was really nice."

"Just really nice?" asked Joe, sceptically.

"So, ok. It's like the wine and everything, just the fucking best I ever had. Open another packet."

Joe got another packet from the cupboard and opened it. He took one bite and was impressed with the texture of the biscuit. It was in the second bite he enjoyed the flavour.

Taking a sip of the coffee, Lilly smiled looking at the cup. "Wow. It just keeps getting better," she said.

Rich flavours rolled over Joe's tongue, as he quickly followed Lilly in tasting the coffee. He let out a satisfied sigh. The wolves' ears perked up when they sensed Joe and Lilly's pleasure, and they started to sniff the air. Noticing their curiosity, Joe reset the coffee machine, and collected the coffee in bowls. The wolves gathered around the bowls and lapped up the coffee. When they had finished, they looked up at Joe and barked their pleasure. They jumped up to lick the two humans' faces, and then ran out of the house playing.

"Well goodbye," said Joe.

"That was sudden," observed Lilly.

Joe shrugged and asked, "Want another cup?"

"Oh yeah," replied Lilly.

They went outside onto the patio to drink their coffees. They were sat in the garden seats just trying to work out what the strange things they saw high up in the air were, when Joe noticed one of the bushes at the far end of the clearing, before the forest proper started, shake. He craned his neck to see if he could tell what was in the bush. Standing up with his eyes fixed on the bush, he walked towards it and stopping a few feet away from it, he stopped and shouted, "Who's there? Show yourself!"

The head of a woman popped up over the bush. Her long face was blackened as if she had been up a chimney, with her big eyes standing out brightly against the soot around them. Her hair was scorched and disheveled. She came out into the open, and Joe looked up to her face. She was slender and very tall, and dressed like she had been out on safari, in knee length khaki shorts and shirt, with ankle boots and thick socks that went up to her knees. Her clothes were scorched and tattered in random patches. Lilly joined them, intrigued by the dishevelled and charred woman.

The woman looked around, and said, "I see you're new," in what Joe thought was a posh British accent.

Joe was not sure what to make of the woman, but he answered the stranger. "Yes," he said. "Who are you?"

"My name's Charlotte," was the chipper sounding reply. "And it's a good thing I found you."

"Why?"

She lowered her head, and Joe and Lilly automatically leaned in closer. "To warn you," said Charlotte, her voice dropping, suggesting danger. Curious, Charlotte's head popped up to quickly check no one else was around, Joe and Lilly automatically straightened and looked around with her. Charlotte lowered her head and Joe and Lilly leaned in again. "This place, the afterlife," she said, almost in a whisper. "It's run by demons,"

"What?" asked Joe, frowning with scepticism.

"Demons. You know what demons are don't you?"

"Demons?" said Joe, scornfully.

"I say keep your voice down old man. There's no need to be tetchy," said Charlotte, popping her head up and looking around again. Lilly and Joe couldn't help looking around as well.

"What happened to you?" asked Lilly, looking at the burnt clothing and soot about her face.

Charlotte looked down at herself. "Ah," she said smiling. "The price of freedom. One must suffer for it."

"Holy shit!" Lilly's eyes popped open. "Were you a suicide bomber?" Then she laughed a little nervously.

"Suicide bomber? What's one of those?"

"You don't know what a suicide bomber is?" said Lilly.

"No, I don't. But let me think." Charlotte tapped the tip of her forefinger against her chin for a moment. "I'm thinking it's like a suicide mission?"

Lilly shrugged, nodded and muttered, "No shit Einstein."

"Einstein? Who's Einstein? I'm sure I've heard that name before. But never mind that, I was on Suicide Bomber."

Charlotte started thoughtfully before getting rapidly more excited, "So it's someone on a suicide mission. Yes! Of course, a suicide bomber is on a suicide mission blowing themselves up to destroy their enemy. Am I right?" she asked wide eyed.

Lilly glanced at Joe. "Fuck! I guess it depends on your point of view."

"Crikey, a bit of a potty mouth there. A lady of quality shouldn't speak like that you know."

"Fuck you," said Lilly.

"Ah," sighed Charlotte. She straightened and looked up through the trees saying "Well, must say, suicide bomber sounds like a noble way to go."

"Noble?" Joe laughed. "There's nothing noble about a suicide bomber."

"Why ever not? What could be more noble than to die fighting your cause, destroying as many of your enemy as you can? I wish I could have had such an end," said Charlotte gazing dreamily into the distance. "For queen and country." She pumped a fist.

"What about walking into a train station, or on a plane and blowing yourself up?" Joe was becoming incensed by the stranger. "What do you think of that?"

Charlotte was unperturbed by Joe's frustration. "I suppose if an enemy was charging across it, and you were to charge into the middle of them. Well, cripes that would be something, eh?"

"What?" said Joe, confused.

"If your enemy is charging at you across a plain, and you charge in and stop them by blowing yourself up. Wouldn't that be a heroic way to go? Imagine if you could take out a whole bunch of them. Stop their attack. Make a real difference to the war effort."

"No! An aeroplane!" Joe was starting to get exasperated.

"Hey calm down," said Lilly. "It's not her fault she doesn't know what you're talking about."

"Oh, I see," said Charlotte. "Yes, I've heard of those."

"Wow, when did you die?" asked Lilly.

"1824. A year I shall never forget," sighed Charlotte, with a drop of the shoulders.

"Bad, huh?" asked Lilly.

"Can we stop jumping around from subject to subject here?" said Joe. He turned to Charlotte. "I apologise for my frustration, but what did you mean about the warning and the demons?"

"Oh yes," said Charlotte, crouching with some sense of urgency, her voice dropping towards a hush once again. "Now listen. The demons are the ones in charge. Don't be fooled by them and their friends."

Joe spread his arms and asked, "Are you trying to tell me we're in hell? This does not look like hell to me."

"Looks can be deceptive," said Charlotte. "This is but a veil, and the true evil lies beneath."

"Well, we were having coffee. Why don't you join us and tell us all about it?" asked Lilly.

Charlotte suddenly stood upright looking around over Joe and Lilly's heads. "What?" asked Joe. "What is it?"

Charlotte squatted lower, and in a quieter whisper said, "They're here." She looked at Lilly. "Coffee would be wonderful young lady, if only to listen to the delightful inflections of your wavering voices."

Lilly was unsure what to say. Joe squinted suspiciously.

"Remember you never saw me," continued Charlotte. "This never happened. We'll meet again. Trust no one."

Lilly and Joe heard Dude calling out to them. He was coming around from the dining room end. They turned and called to him, and when they turned back Charlotte was disappearing into the trees.

"Should we tell them?" asked Lilly.

"No," said Joe. "Let's keep this to ourselves until we know more."

"Alright."

"Jah," said Dude, cheerily walking onto the patio. He gave Lilly a hug and a kiss on the cheek. Dan waved a free hand. He had the butt of a joint in his mouth and his other hand searched through his pockets. He found his lighter and before lighting the joint he took it out of his mouth and asked in his deep southern accent, "Y'all have a good night?"

Lilly spoke first. "We made the best we could out of it," she said. "The wine was amazing, and your joint was smooth."

Dan smiled and put his joint back into his mouth and lit it.

"But you're not going to believe what happened this morning," continued Lilly. Joe looked at her wondering if she was about to talk about Charlotte.

Dude and Dan answered together, "What?"

"Wolves!" Lilly clapped her hands. "Joe falls over me and I sit up, expecting trouble and what do I see? I nearly shit myself. There's a fucking pack of wolves all around me. And thank God they were friendly. They sat with us, and they came in the house, and they ate the biscuits and they loved the coffee. Then they left jumping and playing. It was fucking wonderful."

Joe smiled, nodding his head. "That's right," he said. "Wolves. Amazing creatures."

Dude and Dan laughed. "So, they bring y' joy. They make y' friends," said Dude.

"I'm surprised they didn't tear up the house," said Dan.

"They've done that before?" asked Lilly.

"Many times," said Dan.

"Will they come back?" asked Lilly.

"If they like you," said Dude.

Lilly beamed with delight.

"That pack's been roaming around here for centuries," said Dan.

Joe snorted. "Sure."

"What's that supposed to mean?" asked Dan taking offence at Joe's derision.

Lilly answered whilst Joe paused. "He still believes he's dreaming all this."

"We've been through all this already," Joe dismissed the subject with a wave of his hands. "Let's just get on with why you're here."

"Y' still on that trip man?" said Dude.

Joe pursed his lips before he blurted, "Look none of this fits the teachings I grew up with. Or for that matter the teachings of lots of other faiths. I mean come on! A dope smoking Rastafarian is who greets me when I die? No offence, but really?"

Dude was untroubled by Joe's words. "Joe man, it ain't no business o' mine what y' believe, but y' got t' trust what y' can see," said Dude. He raised his palms up to his face breathing in, "What y' can smell. What y' can hear. What y' can touch." He put his hands on Joe's shoulders, and looked into his eyes. "What your heart tells y'."

Joe rolled his shoulders, and shook off Dude's hands. "Well maybe I'm in a coma, in a hospital, and all of this is my subconscious."

"Maybe," smiled Dude. "Maybe all them stories y' hear are the dreams, the hopes o' them clinging on t' life," he spread his hands out, "'n' reality's greater than all o' them."

Dan laughed. "Whatever this might be, try not to put a downer on it friend. You got to get out and explore your imagination."

"True man," said Dude, laughing gently. "As long as your here, make the most o' the time." He turned to Lilly. "Now lady, is there any more o' that coffee, it smells real fine?"

Lilly smiled, "I bet there is. But Joe's the one who knows how to work the machine."

Lilly, Dude and Dan started walking towards the house. Dan turned to Joe. "Well come on," he said. "You're the man to work the machine."

Muttering under his breath Joe followed them.

They returned to the patio with the coffees, and as they drank the coffee Dude suggested, "Take a walk man," he said. "Y' never know where y' might end up."

"A walk?" said Joe.

"Walk wherever y' want," said Dude.

"I'd like to see my daughter, and my grandson," said Lilly.

"So go there lady," said Dude. "Lot o' people visitin' the livin'. But take heed, the livin' can't see y'."

"Not strictly true," said Dan.

Dude was irritated by Dan's comment. "It's a rare thing man."

"Now don't be telling her half-truths Dude," said Dan.

Dude's face twisted and he reluctantly explained. "It ain't a half truth. Them that can see y' are few lady," he said. Then he warned, "So don't be getting your hopes up now. This boy be messing with y'."

"I'll have less of the boy shit, Dude," said Dan directly.

Lilly did not hear the point about the small possibility. "They could see me?" she asked. Dude's shoulders dropped and he let out a deep sigh. He turned to look at Dan and Dan simply shrugged his shoulders, feigning innocence with a roguish smile.

Joe asked, "How small is this possibility?"

"Very small," said Dan. "So small it's not worth mentioning."

"Y' ever see a ghost?" asked Dude.

"No," said Joe.

"That's 'cos it's a rare thing. If y' ever saw one for real, y' know it. There ain't no doubtin' it," said Dude.

"I definitely have to see my family," said Lilly.

"Well alright," said Dan. "We'll take you."

With genuine surprise Dude exclaimed, "We will?"

"Sure, why not?" said Dan.

Dude was wide eyed. "What y' rolling these days?" he asked.

Dan laughed. "Come on," he said and turned to leave. Lilly sprang up.

"Now?" Joe did not want to leave until he had drunk his coffee and waved his mug in front of his face. It was worth savouring.

"Yes man," agreed Dude. "Be a shame t' leave this fine coffee, and on such a beautiful morning." He lowered himself into one of the seats and took a sip, before putting his hat on the table and leaning back to look across the valley.

They joined Dude, and Dan sat down, sat back and reached into his pocket.

Chapter 5

Walking was how one travelled in the afterlife, which Joe was surprised by. Especially if this was his own fantasy, then why hadn't he fantasized a jet car? Or teleportation? He didn't mind since he didn't feel weary at any time, and the walk was beautiful and he was glad to take the time to appreciate the scenery.

The walk was beautiful even as they wandered into clouds, and as the clouds faded, they were walking on a track, which became a path, onto a pavement by a road, and they were back in the city. Joe could smell and feel the particulates in the air. He covered his mouth, overwhelmed by the contrast to the place he had just left. He could make out the gutters too, and what came in on the wind.

They were in a neighborhood that Joe did not recognize, with poorly maintained old apartment blocks.

Lilly was looking down a road to a particular building. "Why are we here?" she asked. "This is my place, no one'll be here."

"I beg to differ," said Dude, and pointed to Lilly's

building. A couple was coming out of it with a little boy, carrying boxes.

When Lilly got closer and saw her grandson, the joy rose up in her and she immediately dashed down the road.

"What's his name?" asked Joe, when they reached the building.

"Cloud," said Lilly.

"Cloud?"

Lilly was offended. "What's wrong with Cloud?" she asked.

Joe raised his hands. "Nothing," he said.

The family were going back into the building and Lilly followed them. As they walked up the stairs, Cloud asked, "Why are we taking grandma's stuff? Won't she get mad?"

His father was exasperated. "Because she's gone away, Cloud. She's left us for good."

Cloud began to sob, and his father realised his mistake. "I'm sorry son. I shouldn't have said it like that."

Cloud's sobbing grew stronger. "But why can't she come back?" he demanded.

Cloud's father did not answer instead he picked up Cloud and took him up the stairs to a landing with a door at either end of a short corridor. The walls and fixings needed updating, wallpaper was peeling in random spots along the edges of the wall, and the carpet was worn away along the centre, with the colours completely gone.

The door to Lilly's apartment was open and led into the single space making up the living room at one end, the dining and then the kitchen, with the doors to the bedroom and bathroom to the back. Joe immediately noticed that despite the furniture being mismatched, with dining chairs from different tables and living room seats that appeared to have been added from different sources over time, there was the sense of a certain eclectic style about the arrangement. The shelves had a variety of knickknacks, and various books. Joe looked over the collection of books and was quietly impressed by the selection.

Posters were hung on new wallpaper, and overall the ambience was thoughtful and energetic. There were a few family pictures scattered around, and a lot of the drawers and cupboards were open and empty.

"What's your son-in-law's name?" asked Joe.

Lilly smiled. "Joseph," she said. "But he's not my son-in-law, they're not married," said Lilly.

"Very modern," said Joe. "And your daughter's name?"

Before Lilly answered Joseph called out, "Willow? Have you got a minute hon?" Lilly looked around eager to see her daughter.

"Yes," said Willow from the bedroom. "What's up?"

"It's time to have another chat with Cloud," said Joseph.

Willow walked into the main room, and sighed. "Oh man," she said. "It is?" She had obviously been crying.

"There she is," said Lilly proudly.

Willow walked over to Joseph and took Cloud so his face was directly in front of hers. He had wiped the tears, but his cheeks were still damp, and he sniffled.

"Oh dear," said Willow. "I guess we're all upset today."

"He wants to know why Grandma can't come back," said Joseph.

"Oh wow, he's asking the easy ones today, huh?" said Willow.

They all took a seat close together to talk. Lilly and Joseph watched with Dude and Dan as Cloud listened to his parents.

"Now honey," said Willow. "You know what I told you before. She can't come back."

"Why not? Is she angry with us?"

"Oh no honey. She could never be angry with you. Grandma had an accident and she got knocked out of her body, by a bad driver."

Joe grimaced.

Cloud tried to understand what his mother was telling him. "Grandma got knocked out of her body?" he asked.

"Yes dear," said Willow.

"So why doesn't she get back in?" asked Cloud.

"Because she can't," said Willow. "Once she's out, she can't go back in."

"But why?" insisted Cloud. "How did she get in before?"

"That's a good question dear," said Willow. "But that was when she was little and she was just born."

Dan laughed. "The people on this world are so clueless."

"Not now man," said Dude.

Joseph stepped in. "Her body is too broken for her to go back in, son. The doctors can't mend her."

"Oh," said Cloud, with a quizzical look.

"You remember we're going to that church tomorrow?" asked Willow.

Cloud nodded.

"Well, we're going to bury her body. You can say goodbye to her then."

"Will grandma be there?" asked Cloud quickly excited.

"Maybe," said Joseph.

"Cool," said Cloud. "I can't wait to see her. Maybe I could convince her to stay."

"Oh well you know, she might not want to be seen," said Willow.

"Or might not even be there," said Joseph.

Cloud's face dropped and he asked, "Why?"

Willow and Joseph looked at one another, realising they were on the verge of making everything unnecessarily complicated.

"Can I be there, at the funeral?" asked Lilly.

"Of course," said Dude.

"Well, honey," said Willow. "It's strange but true, when you leave your body, people who are still in their bodies can't see the people who've left their bodies."

Cloud thought about what he was being told. "So, if I leave my body, I can see grandma?"

Joseph quickly jumped in, "You can't leave your body son. If you did that, we couldn't see you, and well you might not be able to get back in. It's all very complicated."

"Yes it is, daddy," said Cloud.

"Don't ever try to leave your body honey," said Willow, concerned. "It's very dangerous."

Cloud looked at them both. "So how will grandma know when I say goodbye to her?"

Joseph smiled. "I'm sure she'll hear you."

"She might be listening right now," said Willow.

"I can't hear her," said Cloud. "If she can hear me, I can hear her, and I can't hear her so she's not here."

"Well maybe she's just listening," said Willow. "I bet if you think about her really hard, and say what you want to tell her, then she'll hear it. And you know what?"

"What?"

"You don't even have to say it out loud. You can just say it in your head."

"What!" shouted Lilly, "Christ! Don't tell him that! I can't read his mind!" Then she looked at Dude. "Can I?"

Dude was enigmatically silent.

"That really doesn't help," said Lilly.

"It all depends on what you want," said Dan.

"That's just silly," said Cloud. Joseph smiled.

"Maybe it is," said Joseph. "But tomorrow, you can look at her body and say goodbye. Hopefully she'll be there to hear you."

"Ok," said Cloud. "But I miss her a lot."

"We all do," said Joseph.

"I'm right here baby," said Lilly. Tears were streaming over her cheeks. Joe watched as Lilly reached out to touch her grandson. She brushed his cheek with the back of her hand, and he rubbed the cheek and looked around. Lilly gasped and reached out to her daughter and touched her too, but Willow did not react. Lilly turned away and covered her face as she sobbed. She turned to Joe and shouted. "I had years left in me. Years! I could've seen him grow up." She turned away as her emotions took over her.

"Let's go," said Lilly. "I can't take anymore." She rushed out of the flat.

As they left, Dude asked Joe, "Is this not real, Jonas?" Joe turned his face with anger at Dude.

"Maybe we should take him to his place now," said Dan, lighting another Joint.

A smile slowly spread across Dude's face. "Dan man, sometimes y' got a good idea," he said.

Chapter 6

Oddly discomforted on the journey to his house, Joe reminded himself that this was all a fantasy and his mind was taking him on this journey for a reason. He asked Dude, "How long has it been since I... well got here?"

"Not long," said Dude.

They crossed the city to Joe's home, set in a leafy suburb, in what seemed like a matter of moments. Joe had recognized the neighborhood of Lilly's flat and knew that it would take more than half an hour to get to his house by car.

"You lived here?" said Lilly. "This is very nice."

"Thanks," said Joe, dryly.

A few cars were parked outside Joe's house. "I see my brothers and sister are here. Shem is sitting outside the front door, which is nice."

They all looked at the man, about the same age as Joe, sat on a chair on the front porch. He was quietly looking out across the garden.

"Who is he?" asked Lilly.

"He's a friend from the University. It's right to see

him here. We shared our lunch break almost every day."

The front door was open and they walked into the hallway. The hallway was modest in size and had three doors leading from it. To Joe's surprise there were several people waiting in there, and now looking at him and his companions.

"You know these people?" asked Lilly.

"No," said Joe.

"Why are they all looking at us?"

"You here to see her too?" a woman asked.

Dan laughed.

"Hmm," rumbled Dude.

"See who?" asked Joe. "This is my home. I'm here to see family. Are all of you dead?" He emphasised 'dead'. They all nodded. "So why don't you all go to your own families?"

"Because they can't hear us or see us," said a man sat on the far side. He was much older than Joe, and appeared disgruntled.

"Are you related to her?" asked a middle-aged woman.

"Related to whom?" asked Joe. "Who is this woman you all want to see?"

"They're talkin' about your cousin from France man," said Dude.

"What? Deb?" A smile quickly cut through Joe's confusion.

"Guess so."

Joe addressed the waiting dead, "And you can talk to her?" They all nodded. "Should've known," he concluded after a slight pause.

Joe strode into the living room. Some of his relatives were watching television, looking at phones and tablets, and others were sat at the dining room table. At one end he could see his cousin Deb talking to his sister. She turned when he walked in. She said in a strong French accent, "It's about time you arrived. I must leave tomorrow."

Everyone else looked around. One of the younger men on the sofa, Joe's nephew, Simon said excitedly, "Is he here, aunt Deb?"

"Yes of course he is here. Why else would I say 'It's about time you arrived', and you can see no one?"

"Cool," said the young man. Though Aunt Deb snorted, she was still smiling affectionately at him. She had the classical look of a French dame. Sitting upright and looking elegant in her deep blue, knee-length dress with hints of glitter, and an open neckline. Her hair was tied in a neat bun at the back of her head.

Then Joe's sons came in from another room, and the family gathered around Deb and looked around in Joe's general direction trying to perceive the visitors. Only Deb's eyes were fixed on the group and flicked around to scrutinise Joe's companions.

Deb waved a finger in the direction of Joe's companions. "Who are these others with you?" she asked.

Joe was pulled out of his surprise and introduced his companions. "This is Lilly," he waved a hand at Lilly.

"Hello," said Lilly smiling.

"Bonjour," said Deb.

"This is Dude and Dan."

"Dude? What kind of name is Dude? Is this not a general way of referring to a person, usually a man, and normally by hippies and the like?" asked Deb.

"Maybe so gifted lady, but Dude's the name. The one that make me give it t' me long before man was born," smiled Dude.

"How intriguing," said Deb. "I hope you are not all expecting something from me," said Deb. "I am only here for my cousin."

"You came all this way just for me?" asked Joe.

"Of course I come. Would you not do the same for me."

"You have a lot of faith in me," said Joe. Deb smiled. He would have gone to France for her. "And you can see me?"

"I told you many times I have always been able to see the dead. But you are always the sceptic. Most strange."

"I'm sorry," said Joe.

"As you should be," said Deb. She turned to the boys in the room. "Tell Shem his friend is here."

Simon ran off to the front of the house. Meanwhile other members of Joe's family gathered around Deb.

Simon ran back into the room. "He says to ask Joe does he remember how much he owes him for lunch."

Deb looked at Joe inquisitively. "Tell him I don't owe him anything," said Joe. "Remind him he invited me to lunch. He owes me forty two fifty."

Deb relayed the message to the boy who ran off again.

Joe smiled. "I'm really pleased to see you," he said to Deb.

"So why are these people with you?"

"What's it like Joe?" asked Joe's brother, Ash.

"Eh!" snapped Deb. "Do not interrupt Ash."

Ash turned away sheepishly.

Deb returned her gaze to Joe and his companions. "Now. Explain," she said.

Joe turned to his companions. "The two gentlemen are my guides. They met Lilly and I when we... died."

"You died together?" asked Deb.

"Who died together?" Joe's sister, Vana, asked.

"Lilly and Joe," said Deb.

"Who's Lilly?"

"I think that was the name of the poor woman who was killed in the accident as well," said Ash. "Lillian something."

Simon had run back in from outside and was looking for an opportunity to convey Shem's reply. "What is it Simon," asked Deb.

"Shem wants to ask uncle Joe, what's it like?" said Simon.

"Sacre bleu!" Deb then went into a series of further French expletives.

Joe was enjoying seeing his cousin. "Deb you always lifted my heart. I am so happy to remember you now."

Deb stopped talking, looked straight into Joe's eyes, and asked suspiciously "Happy to remember me? Do you not believe you are dead?"

Lilly laughed and commented, "He thinks we're all part of his imagination."

"Do not tell me," said Deb. "He thinks he is in a coma, or some such?"

"Oh, you know him well."

"But of course, we grow up together as children." Deb laughed. "Always he was the doubter," she said.

"This is a dream because you are so far away, and it's too good to be true. I mean think about it, I come back to my own Siva and my cousin Deb is here, who can speak to the dead."

"You think you are the only one to do this? To return to your famille?"

Joe looked confused.

"Why there are people in your hallway? They are here to see their famille, and their friends. For their Funeral's. Many of the dead return for such things. Why do you think your mama come to me? And your papa? You are not so unique."

A thoughtful silence fell across the group, and it was broken by a young voice. "What shall I tell Shem?" asked Simon.

Deb was suddenly irritated. "Mon dieu! Tell that

orthodox fool to get in here so he may hear with everyone else."

Simon looked nervous. "Alors," said Deb, "I will get him myself." She got up to get Shem. When she entered the hallway, those waiting spoke up and Deb could be heard shouting. "Silence, silence! I will deal with you when I am ready." The waiting spirits fell silent.

Joe's second brother, Tad asked of the others around him, "This is strange. I mean is he really here?"

"Deb isn't crazy," said Vana. "I believe her, and if he is here, he can possibly hear you, even if you can't hear him."

"Yeah," said Ash. "She's telling us what he's saying, but not what we're saying to him."

The assembled family members looked at one another and around the room. Dude and Dan sniggered.

"You know," said Ash. "Just think, we can't see them, we can't hear them. What if the dead are around all the time? I mean you could be anywhere, doing whatever you might want to do, and they could be right there watching, listening."

Once again, the assembled family members fell silent and looked around the room, this time uncomfortably. Dude and Dan's sniggering grew more intense.

"Oh stop it," said Vana. She was uncertain as she then said, "They don't hang around doing that."

"Hey, that's the kind of thing mum would do. You know how she was always wanting to know everything," said Tad.

Everyone, including Joe, looked at Tad. Joe told himself he shouldn't worry this was a fantasy after all.

Dan and Dude started to laugh. Joe turned to them. "Something you'd like to share?" he asked.

"Not a thing," said Dan, and looking at Dude continued to laugh.

Deb came back into the room dragging Shem in with her. He was obviously unhappy about entering the house. "You know this better not get back to the rest of the community. There'll be consequences."

"Stop with this complaining and sit down. Your friend thinks you are not real," said Deb.

As Shem sat down with the family at the end of the dining table, he was surprised by what Deb had to say. "What do you mean," he asked. "Does he think he's dreaming? And we're all in his dream?"

"He believes he is in a coma."

"Oh." Shem turned to look to the other end of the dining table. He did not look directly at Joe, and Deb corrected him. Though now he appeared to be looking straight through Joe at the wall.

Shem continued, speaking as clearly as he could. "I'm not a dream Joe. You're dead, there's no way you could survive that accident. That truck hit you on the driver's side. And that poor woman who got caught by your car. What a mess." Shem finished by covering his face with his hand and turning away.

Joe paced back and forth, before he turned back to Shem and said, "Well that's just what I expect to be told. That's all anyone's said, but it can't be right.

None of the things I would hope for are here. I mean these guys are smoking cannabis for god's sake." He pointed at Dude and Dan, who spluttered with mirth.

"He cannot hear you," said Deb. She turned to Shem and passed on Joe's comments, though not as emotionally as Joe had expressed them.

"They're smoking cannabis in the afterlife?" asked Ash.

"Yeah. How can this be real if they're doing that? What kind of death is this?"

"Does it feel real?" asked Shem.

"Your senses can be confused," said Joe.

"But it feels real," said Lilly to Joe. "It's like I know it's real. Why don't you feel that?"

"The mind plays tricks."

Shem looked to Deb, Deb turned to him and said, "Joe is arguing with Lilly, the woman who was killed in the accident. She says it is real. The other two are just watching and, I believe the word is sniggering."

"The woman who Joe killed is here?" asked a shocked Shem.

"See, even your friend thinks you killed me," said Lilly.

Deb nodded to Shem, answering his question. Shem turned back in the general direction of where he thought Joe was. "That must be terrible Joe," said Shem.

Joe stepped back to where Shem was looking, and faced his friend. "You have no idea," he said from the far wall.

"This is…, how you say, frustrating," said Deb. She pointed to a seat at the other end of the table. "S'asseoir. They will have a place to look."

Joe went to pull the chair back. He felt the chair, and the pressure he put on it, but when he tried to apply the necessary pressure to move the chair his hand passed through it. Joe looked at his hand, shocked. "That was strange," he said. He had felt the chair as he had passed through it, in a way he was unsure he would have imagined.

"Y'ain't got the power man," said Dude.

"No, but I do," said Dan. He grabbed the chair and pulled it out. The assembled family members and Shem gasped and moved in closer together, having seen the chair apparently move on its own. Their reaction served to amuse Dan more.

Dude sucked in air through his teeth, his mood had switched from mirth to anger. "Man y' pushin' it now," he said. "Stop your messing around! There'll be trouble."

Joe eyed Dan suspiciously as he sat down. "Better?" he asked Deb.

"Much," replied Deb. She looked at Lilly and the others. "You may sit also," she said.

Joe's family gasped again when three more chairs were pulled out, and Lilly giggled while Dan laughed. Joe could feel Dude's glare, even though it was directed at Dan.

Vana looked at Joe's chair and tentatively said, "We

all miss you, Joe." Then her face changed into one of confusion and she said, "This is weird knowing you're gone but you're here."

"That's true," said Ash. "Knowing you're still out there makes your dying a little less painful, and I'm glad for that. I mean, I suppose we can always meet in the afterlife. Right?"

"Remember, he doesn't believe he's dead," said Tad.

"Is mum there," asked Sam, Joe's older son.

With sadness Joe replied, "I haven't seen her yet."

Both of his sons were disappointed, Eitan visibly more so.

"What kind of dream is this?" asked Shem. "You have to spend time with the person you killed, but you can't meet your dead wife? That sucks."

"Tell me about it," said Joe.

"Sucks for me too," said Lilly.

"He agrees," said Deb. "As does Lilly."

"Look, I've got to ask," said Lilly to Deb. "Can you talk to my daughter for me?"

"I do not do that," said Deb dismissing the request with a wave of her hand.

"Oh please. I really need to tell her and my grand-son that everything's ok."

With a stern look, Deb replied, "What do you think? If I do this then I will have a queue of the dead at my door. And the living, they think I am crazy. Look at them out there now." She pointed at the hallway. "Pour quoi? Because I avoid one and he realizes I can see him. You think I have nothing better to do with my life? You cannot even pay. I am only here for my cousin."

"My daughter can pay," said Lilly.

"If I ask for money, then definitely she will not believe me."

Lilly said, distressed, "You're helping Joe."

"Of course. He is famille. I come for him. He is like a close brother to me. All of these people are close to me, we all grow up together, for many years."

Whilst Deb looked at Lilly, the family looked at Deb and Lilly's chair. They were hearing half the conversation and Ash understood enough to say to Lilly's chair, "Lilly, Deb's family, but even we always kind of wondered how real this ability of aunt Deb's was."

Deb was not shocked. Mockingly "Quoi?" she said. "Non. Vraiment?"

"Sorry," said Tad. "We never saw your ability like this. With this conversation and with the chairs moving like that, it just brought home how real it is."

"But what about the messages from your mama, and your papa?" asked Deb.

"Yeah," Ash rubbed his collar, "they were difficult to dismiss."

Deb stood up. "I know of your scepticism," she said. She looked at Joe. "And what about you? Even now you are so doubtful you believe you are dreaming."

"Uh well," said Joe, quickly. "I never thought you were crazy."

"We don't think you're crazy Deb," said Vana.

"Then what? Maybe you think I am very creative?" said Deb.

Vana squirmed. "Well, we don't anymore."

Joe sighed. The rest of his family looked worried. Dan was covering his mouth, to hide his amusement. Dude tugged on a reefer.

"You, Deb," said Joe. "You were as much my sister as Vana, and the best of friends." Deb sat down. "When your family moved to France, I missed you so much. Your letters were wonderful, and I looked forward to them all, especially when you wrote to me about the strange people you spoke to. Holidays when we met were the best. You livened the atmosphere where ever you went. Those memories come back to me now as clear as the day they were made. They make me so happy." As Joe spoke Deb began to smile. "I had my doubts and you always knew that, I made no secret of them to you. But I could never prove you wrong. And when you sent me the notes from my mother and my father, I was touched and my heart was comforted. Despite what I may or may not have believed.

"You know Sarah was a little jealous of you for a while? Only a little and not for long."

The rest of the family's eyes flicked between the chair and Deb, and as she smiled, they began to relax.

"You know she came to love you too. Always surprised me you never sent a note from her."

"You say such nice things," said Deb. "But still, I sense you are not yet believing. You are still doubtful, despite the feelings that run through you now."

Joe looked down to the table.

"It is ok," said Deb. She looked at Dude and Dan. "I am sure it is not the first time this has happened." Dude simply smiled, and Dan was unaware of Deb whilst he drew on another joint. She looked back to Joe. "Time will bring the answers you need."

"What did he say?" asked Ash.

"Nothing that concerns you," Deb told him sternly.

"What about mum and Dad?" he asked.

Joe shook his head. "No," said Deb.

"What about uncle Bart?" asked Tad.

Joe shook his head. The family looked perplexed.

"What does that mean?" asked Shem.

"It just means I haven't been in the... here for long," said Joe. "Maybe when I look around a little, I'll see them."

"But won't they be figments of your imagination?" asked Ash. "You know, if you think this is all a dream."

Joe tried to think of a way to explain.

"Unless of course, you're hedging your bets," said Tad.

"Yeah. That would make sense. Be just like Joe," said Ash.

"Play along, just in case," said Tad.

Joe was shocked. "Is that what you think? I'm hedging my bets?"

"Doesn't matter what I think," said Tad. "Only you. If you're right of course."

"You can't blame him for being doubtful," said

Shem. "I mean, I know he's dead, I walked past the accident on my way to the University. But it doesn't sound like he's experiencing anything enlightening." He turned to Joe's chair. "Have you learnt anything, Joe?"

They talked for some time more, with Deb conveying Joe's words to his family. When they were almost done, Vana said, "Thank you Deb. You've comforted us again, in our time of grief."

"Please answer mine," said Lilly.

"They will not believe me," said Deb.

"Maybe Dude or Dan could move something and convince them?" said Lilly.

Dude quickly raised his hand before anything more could be said. "No lady, please don't ask that." He pointed at Dan, "This one should not 'a' moved those chairs. This is bad." Dan was slouched back surrounded by smoke. "You see your causin' trouble again." But Dan didn't hear him, looking distant. Dude hit him on the shoulder, and Dan jerked as he was snapped back to the present, and looking around asked, "What?" Dude shook his head and turned away.

"I sense you are something other than the deceased," said Deb to Dude. "Why can you not help?"

"Lady, y' got a gift, but for deep reasons the gift is rare," said Dude. "Those deep reasons are why I can't do anythin' like this fool done." Deb seemed to understand.

"Wow man," said Herschel, one of the nephews.

"This is so awesome." He was holding a phone in front of his face with the camera on the group around the table.

"What are you doing, Herschel?" asked Deb.

"I got the whole thing aunt Deb," said Herschel.

"Oh, mon dieu," said Deb. "It will help nothing," she said.

"Are you kidding? When people see those chairs move, it'll go viral. Doesn't matter what anyone believes."

"Hey we're not giving you permission to use our images or any of this," said Sam.

"What? Oh, come on, Sam," said Herschel stopping the recording. "There's money in this."

Deb tutted. She sat down, and looked at Vana. "A cup of tea will be very nice now," she said.

Vana got up immediately "Coming right up," she said as she skipped to the kitchen.

"And also paper and pen," said Deb looking at Ash. Ash sprang out of his seat and went off to Joe's office. She looked at Lilly, "I will write a note with your words, and I will send it to your famille. As I will for those in the hallway, but that is all. My cousin Joe has softened my mood, and you shall benefit."

Deb turned to Dude. "I have seen many of the dead. Tell me, why you smoke so much cannabis?"

Dude looked at Deb, and before he could say anything, Dan replied, "Why not?" After a moment of thought, Deb shrugged.

Lilly was grateful for Deb's generosity and the rest

of the family sat down to share time with Joe. Sam and the others agreed to let Herschel upload his video on certain conditions.

Chapter 7

Joe and Lilly were lost in their own thoughts as they walked back to the house. They were oblivious to all that was around them, failing to observe the people that were on the streets or the change in the path as they walked into the forest, and the route that Dude and Dan had taken, or the objects in the sky above, or the sounds and sights of the wildlife, and occasional humans, so much so that when they looked up, they were at their house.

Dude and Dan left them at the door. Dude promised to return and take Lilly to her funeral.

After sitting in his room thinking about his experience with Deb, Joe decided to go down and have a drink. He went outside to find Lilly already there.

Despite her anger, Lilly welcomed Joe's company, and for a while they were sat in silence.

"Have you noticed how many stars there are?" asked Joe.

"There are a lot of stars," said Lilly.

"But it's still day time and the sky is blue," said Joe.

"Yeah," said Lilly. "Weird."

Joe laughed.

"It's so quiet out here. Isn't it wonderful?" she asked.

Joe considered. "Why aren't there more people?" he asked.

"What do you mean?"

"Think about it. How many people have lived and died over the centuries? And we've hardly seen any. How many billions? They should be everywhere, as far as the eye can see."

"I don't know," she said. "How big is the afterlife? How big is space?"

They both turned their gaze back to the stars.

The light faded quickly and soon they were breathing clean, cool air drifting down to the valley from the hills and mountains.,

"I guess you have a point," said Joe.

Lilly reached into a pocket. "How about a smoke?" she asked holding up a joint.

"Why not."

"Oh yeah."

Joe didn't know if he was really experiencing the effects of marijuana, but he liked whatever it was he was feeling. They were both gazing at the stars in silence when they heard rustling from the edge of the forest.

"There's someone out there," said Joe.

"I hear it too," said Lilly. "Do you want to go and have a look? Maybe it's Charlotte. She did say she'd be back."

Joe was not sure, even though the daylight was gone he could see clearly, but it was a forest and he was still a city man. He instinctively crouched and peered into the bushes.

Joe edged to the end of the open space behind the house and then cautiously ventured in the direction of the noise. He looked back and saw Lilly was not behind him.

"Are you going to stay there?" he asked.

"You look like you can take care of yourself," said Lilly. "I'm sure there's nothing dangerous out there."

"There were a pack of wolves before. Or did you forget?"

"Oh, come on. You can't use them as an excuse. They were gentle and wouldn't hurt a fly. Anyway, what are you worried about this is your fantasy land."

Joe huffed and stood up straight. "You're right," he said. "Damn it. What am I frightened of?" He walked towards the noise and as he got closer, he noticed the rhythmic nature of the rustling and as he neared the source, just before he pulled back the leaves and branches, he heard the clearly recognizable moans of sexual ecstasy.

"Oh my," he said.

It was a young couple who were unaware of him until he spoke. They were entwined and naked, moving rhythmically together. Rather than be upset they looked over and smiled. "Oh hi," said the man. "How are you doing?"

Joe had his mouth hung open, and was not sure what to say. "Uh fine," he managed eventually.

"Wow," moaned the woman. "Look at his skin. The lines. You look like you just arrived." She moaned. "Let me touch you. Feel you."

"That will be quite alright," said Joe. "Sorry to have disturbed you." He quickly turned about and headed back to the house.

When he had returned to the clearing, Lilly stared at him, unsure of what to make of the look on his face. "What is it?" she asked. "What was out there?"

"Oh, just some young couple, doing what comes naturally."

Lilly thought about what Joe had said, then she smiled wickedly. "No way!" she said. "Were they hot?"

Joe looked at her surprised. "I can't say, I was rather shocked."

"Oh, come on. I bet you noticed her."

Joe took a sip of his drink and said, "She was a perfectly agreeable looking woman. Quite young, and she wanted to touch me. Oddly."

"Really? She wanted you to join in?"

"I don't think she wanted me to join in. I think she was just fascinated by my skin, said something about the lines on my face."

Lilly laughed. "Still, I can't get away from the sex you've imagined so far."

Joe fidgeted in his seat and poured himself another drink.

Some while later, the rustling was closer, and the young couple were approaching Joe and Lilly, straightening their clothes as they walked. "Is that the couple?" whispered Lilly. She heard a quiet, "Mm hmm."

The woman's clothing was beautiful, made of bright silks, embroidered with gold thread and inlaid with sparkling stones, that glittered even in the light of the night. The man was tying his wraparound pantaloons, with a short sleeved white shirt under an embroidered waistcoat of matching colours to his partner's.

"Hi," they said and Joe uttered, "Hi."

Lilly replied, "Did you have fun?" laughing.

"Yes we did," said the young woman in an extremely cheerful tone.

Joe was silent.

"Why don't you sit down and have a drink?" said Lilly. Joe was surprised by Lilly's invitation but kept his silence.

"That would be great," said the young man.

Whilst the couple got chairs, Joe got up and asked, "Is red wine ok?" They both nodded, and Joe went to get another bottle and glasses. Releasing his breath as he walked.

When Joe returned the couple were smiling and laughing with Lilly. As he gave them their drinks Lilly introduced the couple. "This is Ruchika and Varn," she said. "They've been dead a long time."

"What's a long time?" asked Joe.

"Better if we just told you when we died," said

Varn. "Which was 1574 for me and the 14th century for Ruchi. Is that right?"

"Yes, it is," said Ruchi. She turned to Lilly and Joe. "He always forgets the year," said Ruchi.

"Wow," said Joe. "You're looking good, considering you're several hundred years old." He took his seat.

"I've just been telling them about what's been going on recently," said Lilly.

"Anything particular you're interested in?" asked Joe.

"Anything from your recent past," said Ruchika. "We catch up whenever we can."

"Don't you ever go back? To see for yourself, I mean," asked Joe.

"We do," said Varn. "But we haven't done it in a long time."

They drank more wine and Lilly pulled out another joint.

Joe's mind loosened and they spoke and laughed describing the madness of the modern age. In mid laughter, Ruchika leaned over to Joe and said, "Joe, tell us, why do you think this is all a dream?"

Joe shrugged his shoulders. "Were you told the afterlife was going to be anything like this?"

"No," said Ruchika. "I was expecting to experience something like my ancestors had taught us to expect. I expected to be reincarnated. No one told me there would be a choice."

Joe laughed.

Ruchika smiled and had a desirous look, which made Joe uncomfortable again.

"If all this is in your mind," said Ruchika, her voice dropped and she leaned closer to Joe. "Why don't you just enjoy it?"

Joe could feel intense flutters in his stomach and he was gripping the arms of his seat tightly, her sensuality was intoxicating. Leaning back, he said, "Well I may be wrong. Nothing's certain."

Ruchika reached out and put her hand gently on the back of Joe's. Her touch was soft and exciting as it trailed over his skin. His nose filled with her scent and the intensity sent shivers along his back. He turned around to see Lilly leaning back from Varn's approach.

"Well now look here," said Lilly. "This is all moving too fast for me." She backed away from Varn. Joe fell out of his seat. He stood up and together they backed away towards the house.

Ruchika and Varn stood up, their forms sculpted in the light of the night. "We can go as slow as you like," smiled Varn.

"Maybe so," said Lilly. "But I'm not that kind of girl."

"Yeah. I'm not sure I want to be diving in," said Joe. He was unable to ignore the heaving of Ruchika's bosom.

The couple came together putting their arms around each other. "That is so unfortunate," said Ruchika. "You're so delicious."

"Uh huh," said Joe. "So, we'll just go back in now. Please feel free to leave when you're ready."

"Maybe when you're settled in," said Varn, as he turned to Ruchika's neck.

"Don't leave it too long," said Ruchika. Her eyes closed as she offered more of her neck to Varn's lips.

Joe and Lilly turned and walked back to the house with the sound of Ruchika's gasps.

Once they were inside and the glass doors were slid shut, Joe and Lilly looked to see the couple amorously embrace on the garden chair. "That was weird," said Lilly.

"Yes, it was," said Joe.

"He's very handsome," she ventured.

"I suppose."

"And she's incredibly sexy."

"Mm hmm."

"I mean, when was the last time anyone so attractive threw themselves at you?"

"Never," said Joe.

"Really? And the first time it happens you're running away."

Joe looked at Lilly. "You are too."

Unable to look away from the scene unfolding outside, Lilly replied, "I'm starting to wonder if we necessarily did the right thing."

Joe was surprised. "You want to join them?"

"My god that boy has some rhythm."

Irritated, Joe turned away from the view of the

couple on the chair. "If you want to go out and join them, go ahead. It's your choice, but I'm going to bed."

"It's not a dream though, Joe," said Lilly. "You have to admit, this doesn't feel like any dream you've ever had."

Joe said, "Good night, Lilly. See you in the morning."

Chapter 8

Mesmerised by the sound of swaying branches, Joe could also hear birdsong and animals walking through the undergrowth, with the rustle of leaves and the breaking of twigs. It didn't matter how many times he stopped to hear and smell and see all that was around him, he was struck by the symphony that touched his senses.

There was mellow music playing gently in the background, coming from the living room. It was on when he came down. He hadn't bothered to turn it off as he liked it, and the volume, though unbearably loud in the living room, was just right for the kitchen.

Unfortunately, the sandwich he made was not great. The ingredients were fantastic, but the combination just didn't work. It appeared that even in his own fantasy he was terrible at anything to do with combining edible ingredients, even when he didn't need to cook them. He wasn't hungry, he hadn't felt hunger since waking in this creation in his mind. Another reason to believe it a fantasy. He had only made the sandwich for something to do so he gave up and put it aside after the first bite.

He recalled that on many occasions he had absent mindedly burnt eggs. Sarah had often laughed at his failures in the kitchen and she had shared his failures with her friends. He did not mind, as she played along with his jokes, and at parties they made a good double act. He remembered in detail these moments, and the meals Sarah had cooked. Throughout their short life together she had produced wonderful food.

Lilly had gone to her funeral. Joe had met her in the morning and they drank coffee together. He made no mention of the night before, so she ventured, "Weren't you in the least bit tempted?"

"Not at all," said Joe.

Lilly squinted at him and said with an amused smile, "Liar."

Joe grimaced and said, "Alright, I was a little tempted. She was incredibly beautiful."

"And sexy."

"Yes, and sexy."

Joe looked at Lilly and asked, "So did you go out and join them?"

"You tell me," said Lilly. "This is your fantasy."

Joe muttered, "Very good."

"It's a fair point, isn't it Joe? Why don't you know everything that's going on in your dream?"

"What? You never know everything that's going on in your dream."

"Yeah sure," said Lilly. "Why haven't you changed this dream? Why am I still in this house with you?"

"That doesn't always work," said Joe. "Most of the time you're reacting to what's going on. You don't plan a dream. Imagine how boring it would be if you knew everything that was going to happen."

Lilly scoffed. "You are one stubborn man," she said.

"God damn it, Lilly! How many times do I have to state it? How could anyone accept this as the afterlife? Where the people who greet me are smoking drugs. Don't you think the whole dope smoking Rastafarian is something of a cliché?"

Lilly squirmed a little. "Yes, I admit that is a cliché," she said. Her voice rising, she said, "But I am not a fucking figment of your imagination. And you can't deny what your senses tell you."

The argument reached an end with both parties sticking to their beliefs, and Lilly storming off. He was relieved, as he was getting fed up with the question of his belief constantly recuring.

Joe didn't go with Dude and Lilly. He had no interest in going to Lilly's funeral. Instead, he wandered around the outside of the house, and found the bin. There was one large bin and it was on the side of the house, outside the dining room wall, near the external door to the utility room. Looking around Joe didn't see any roads, there were only tracks leading from the clearing the house was built on, so he wondered how the rubbish was collected and by whom.

When Lilly had come back down, she put on the music so it could be heard outside and joined him. She was dressed tastefully in dark clothes appropriate for a funeral.

After some time, Dude arrived without Dan and went with Lilly to her funeral. After they had shared a very sweet tasting bud.

Alone on the patio, Joe was given to wondering once again, why his mind would create Lilly and why he would end up in a house with her. If it was his mind, then she must have represented something important. If he was dead, then Dude was an unfortunate cliché, even with the intelligence and charisma he emanated. Dan was something else. Joe didn't know what to make of a sharply dressed Asian with a vicious undertone to his demeanour. Maybe Charlotte was right and he was a demon. He felt like Dan would happily watch him roasting over a fire, slowly burn and listen to his screams with delight.

The meeting with his family was powerful, and seeing Deb was wonderful. The notes she had sent when his parents passed away told Joe that his father was happy, and that his mother was with his father. Because the note had come from Deb, he sent a reply thanking her. If it had been anyone else, he would have sent a scathing reply, telling them what fools they were, and not to play with people's feelings.

He was a scientist, a physicist to be more precise, and in the opinion of most scientists, religion was a crutch. As much as he had honoured the teachings of his parents, he had not truly believed that there was anything beyond death. Though when his wife Sarah had died, he had had a sense that she was with him for years after. He was convinced that he had felt her presence on several occasions, and it had led him to open his mind and consider possibilities that many of his colleagues considered ridiculous. That feeling that Sarah was with him had eventually passed, and though he attended temple it was only lip service. He went to stay in touch with his community and of course the temple did some good works.

Joe cleared the fresh pile of flyers that had already started to appear, into the pile he had pushed aside earlier, when he had answered the door for Dude.

Out of curiosity he'd taken a handful, gone to the table in the kitchen and laid them out. He was surprised by the variety of services on offer. There weren't just menus from a host of differing styles of cuisine, there were also detective services and therapists. There were suppliers of household goods, and food. He would have expected that all of it would have been better placed in a book indexing the various services. He guessed that the publisher of Yellow Pages had not found traction in the afterlife. But this was Joe's own fantasy and he couldn't help it if he couldn't think of everything. He threw aside the therapists, who asked the questions, in bold and large print, such as, 'Is the afterlife all you hoped for?' Then there was a flyer from a company making flyers, saying, 'Got a great idea? Want to let people know? You need a flyer.

We make and distribute your ideas to billions. Come over and let's talk.'

Joe sighed and decided to have a shower. He stood under the shower feeling the strike of the streams of hot water for a long time. Eventually he came out of the shower and wiping away the humidity looked at his reflection in the mirror. He did not see anything new or different to the man that had the accident. He was still bald and the hair around the sides hadn't gone from white to grey, and the muscles of his body were wiry, and there was loose skin around his waist and hanging from the usual places on his body. His face was lined and showed his years. He told himself the water had wrinkled his skin a little more than usual.

Joe dried off and then took out a pair of jeans and t-shirt. The pile of used clothes was relatively small, there were a good many more fresh clothes still in the cupboards.

Having been advised to walk and discover more of this fantasy, he decided he would see where his feet took him. He put on the walking shoes from the cupboard at the entrance hall, and a waterproof jacket. He took a water bottle from the fridge, telling himself he probably did not need it, but it was better to be cautious, especially since he had little control over this dream.

The sky was blue and bright and there were a few clouds, just perfect for a walk. He went to the hallway cupboard and took a Panama hat.

Walking away from the house, Joe found a path that ran along the edge of the valley. Then Joe had to pause when he thought he saw a man swimming through the air above him. Specifically, the air swimmer was doing the breaststroke. He wondered how he was doing that.

Joe found an open patch of ground, and looked around to see if anybody was about. Certain no one could see him, he thrust his hands upwards and pushed with his legs. It was a short jump, with his landing being exactly where he had stood. He tried again and this time closed his eyes and concentrated hard on leaving the ground and floating up into the air. Nothing happened. He imagined pushing himself away from the ground, this time he lost balance as he landed and almost fell over. Frustrated he went forwards and throwing his arms up, threw his body as well, and fell flat onto the ground.

It hurt to fall on the ground. Joe cautiously stood up, brushed himself off, and checked his surroundings. There was no one around. His body hurt in places where the ground had been harder. Abandoning any further attempts at flight, he returned to his walk, muttering under his breath, "Can't be real. Can't be real."

After some moments, the words were repeated from above in a squawk, "Can't be real. Can't be real." Taking off his hat, Joe looked up. In the tree above him was a parrot. Its colours were vibrant in the backdrop of shadowed green leaves.

"No," said Joe laughing. "It can't be real."

"Can't be real. Can't be real," came a squawk.

Joe looked around and couldn't see anyone nearby.

"Fields of Solitude!" came a shout from behind bushes near the tree.

"Fields of solitude. Fields of solitude," squawked the parrot.

A man popped up from behind the bushes. He was only visible from above the chest. He was covered in long dark hair from his head and face. The man bent down, and when he stood up again, he was holding a rock that was bigger than his hand could wrap around. He took a step, cocked his arm back and flung the rock at the parrot. The rock barely reached the branch the bird was sat on. The parrot watched the arc of the stone as it peaked and came back down with a solid thud, becoming partially buried. The parrot squawked and seemed to be laughing at the stranger's woeful effort.

"You're a stupid bird," shouted the man. "Get away from here."

"Shut up Isaiah. Shut up Isaiah," squawked the parrot.

Joe looked at the man. "Don't you tell me to shut up you stupid bird," shouted Isaiah. "I'll kill you and I'll eat you and throw what's left of you into a deep, dark chasm."

"Shut up Isaiah. Shut up Isaiah," the bird squawked again, followed by what Joe was sure was a laugh.

Isaiah ran out from behind the bushes, completely

naked and covered only by his long hair and beard. None the less Joe could make out musculature and a body that looked like it was made for fighting. "I'm going to make a bow and arrow and kill you, you stupid bird!" He turned to look around the ground. Searching for the materials to carry out his threat.

The parrot squawked, "Already dead. Already dead."

"You'll be a dead dead parrot, you stupid bird!"

"Oh my god," said Joe. "How long have you been here?"

Isaiah stopped and looked at Joe, his face suddenly still and empty. Sounding exasperated, he said, "I don't know. But I see from your youth you must be new."

The parrot squawked and Isaiah's attention snapped back to the bird. He raised a fist to it. "Fields of Solitude you stupid bird. Solitude, why can you not understand?"

The parrot squawked with laughter before it flapped its wings and flew off. "Goodbye Isaiah, goodbye Isaiah," it squawked and laughed.

As it flew out of sight, Isaiah sighed. He smiled and said, "Well goodbye then. A bit sudden all things considered."

Isaiah then turned his attention to Joe. "Who are you?" he asked.

"Joe."

Joe stuck his hand out.

Isaiah stared at the hand. "Do you have a token you wish to share?" he asked.

Confused, Joe withdrew his hand.

"Joe?" said Isaiah. "Can't say I've heard that name before. Which land does it come from?"

"Which land?" said Joe. "That's an odd question."

"Is it?" asked Isaiah. "Why?"

"Nobody says 'which land' anymore," said Joe.

"So, whose kingdom do you come from?"

"Whose kingdom?"

"You're not from a kingdom?"

"There are kingdoms but they don't belong to anyone. At least they're not ruled in the same way. Kingdoms are democracies and then there are republics. There are dictatorships of course, which is probably the same as a kingdom."

As Joe was speaking Isaiah appeared to get distracted, his attention turning to Joe's clothing. He reached out and rubbed the t-shirt between his fingers and thumb. "This material is so soft, yet firm and strong." He tugged on the sleeve, pulling on Joe's shoulder.

"Hey, easy!" said Joe.

"And your feet are covered with the most unusual sandals I have ever seen," continued Isaiah. "What age is it?"

"Age?" Joe sounded confused.

Isaiah, looked at Joe closely. "You really are confused," said Isaiah. "But I suppose you've only recently arrived."

"Look can't you put on some clothes?" demanded Joe.

"Clothes?"

"Yes! You're naked and it's very distracting."

Isaiah looked down at himself and then started to jump and dance. "Does this trouble you?" he laughed. "I was known for my manhood, famed for the number of women I could take in a night."

Joe averted his eyes. "Oh for god's sake stop dancing," he said. He raised his hands to block the view. "Why are you naked anyway? Have I wandered into a nudist camp?"

"Nudist camp?" said Isaiah. He spread his arms, his hands open and turned around saying, "These are the Fields of Solitude. People come here to think, to analyse, to unravel the mysteries of life."

A shout came across the bushes. "Could you keep it down? I'm trying to be solitary over here, and you're very distracting."

"See what I speak of," said Isaiah.

"Yes," came another voice. "Go away so we can be alone. It was bad enough with that parrot."

A stranger stood up in the distance. Joe could barely see his head over the bushes. He was under another solitary tree, with long dark hair. "I hadn't heard another voice for centuries until you came along. Now push off!"

Various voices picked up. "Yeah, push off." "We're trying to contemplate, so go away."

"But I didn't start all this," said Joe. He pointed at Isaiah, "Him and that parrot did."

"Well take him with you," came another shout. Another voice joined in with, "He's been a pain ever since he got here."

"Yeah, take him with you," someone else chimed in. "And his dead parrot."

"Not very friendly, are they?" said Joe.

"Come," said Isaiah. "Let's go. You can tell me what's been happening in the world."

"Before you go," said a woman's voice. "I am curious to know what age it is." A head appeared from behind a bush. Joe couldn't make out a face through the hair that fell over it, in rich dark curls.

"I'm from the twenty first century," said Joe.

Another head popped up, the hair flopped over his face, towards the left of the first head. "What does that mean?" he asked.

"What does it mean? It means the twenty first century in the Christian calendar."

Another head appeared to the right of the first. "What's Christian? Is that the latest empire?" he asked.

Joe did not know where to begin. "To explain that I'd have to know what era you died in."

A fourth head appeared. "Aah, so Christian is not a tribe," she said.

"No," said Joe.

There were a few more 'aahs' from other bushes.

The third head looked across at the second. "I say, is that you Gil?" he asked.

"Yes," said Gil. He moved the hair from over his

eyes, and squinted towards the third head. "Who are you?" he asked.

"It's me, Ty," said the third head, parting the hair in front of his face.

Gil and Ty beamed at each other with recognition, and scampered through the bushes. Emerging from the foliage they rushed across and threw their arms around one another. Joe then realised they were just as naked as Isaiah, with longer hair. He looked away quickly, as their hug appeared to be far longer and more personal than the expectations of normal social protocols.

"Well blow me," said Gil. "Fancy meeting you here."

With their arms over each other's shoulders, Gil and Ty wandered off lost in their own conversation.

The fourth head came out of the bushes, and Joe saw that she too was naked. She was also young and appeared to be in the prime of life.

"These Christians, they came about two thousand one hundred years ago?" she asked.

Joe found himself distracted. He couldn't help no-ticing her large nipples poking out through the long hair. He consciously made the effort to redirect his eyes to her face. "Um yes. Roughly. I'm no expert on ancient history of course," he said. He tried very hard not to look away from her eyes, though he thought they too were exceptionally beautiful.

"I've never even heard of them," she said. "So, I guess I've been here for over two thousand years."

Joe was drawn to the glow of the young woman's

beautifully tanned skin. "Well, you certainly don't look it," he laughed nervously. She smiled sweetly and came closer to Joe. His hairs stood up, and butterflies filled his stomach. His nostrils flared and, for a moment, he appeared to fall into a trance.

Joe pulled himself together. "It's not really called the Christian Calendar, I think it's the Gregorian Calendar, but it's related to the start of Christianity. Around the time of Christ, who supposedly started the religion."

The first head walked over and Joe found himself doubly distracted. He turned to notice Isaiah standing proud with his hands behind his back, smiling happily looking at the ladies.

Isaiah leaned over to Joe. "By the gods, if I'd only known these beauties were so close," he said.

"So, I see," said Joe, his eyes directed at Isaiah's manhood. Isaiah looked down and laughed.

"Christ? Who is Christ?" asked the first head. "And what do you mean 'supposedly'?"

"Well like I said," said Joe, nervously. "History is not really my thing. I believe there's some uncertainty about the life of Jesus."

"Jesus? Who is Jesus?" asked another voice from a bush.

A shout came from the distance. "Will you lot take it somewhere else?" A man popped up, waving his fist at them. In an exasperated voice he shouted, "You've got all of infinity to choose from, so go get lost in it!

This is just like that time that bloody fool fell into my hole."

"Be calm," said Isaiah. "Carry on like that and you shall lose your hair."

"I should be so lucky," shouted the distant man. He looked around, as if he heard a sound, and dropped back behind his bush.

Isaiah turned to the two women, smiling. "Ladies," he said, "I know a place with soft grass and the scent of jasmine in the air, and the sounds of water softly trickling over smooth stones and the music of song-birds. Let me take you there, so I may enhance that beauty with your presence. We could linger, whilst my friend and I answer all your questions as we lye on soft grass."

The ladies smiled at Isaiah. The first one said, "Hmm I think I need to meditate about that."

"Me too," said the second woman. "It might take a while."

Isaiah sighed. "I shall dream you had said yes," he said. The first woman smiled and leaned over to him and whispered in his ear. His eyes widened slowly and a lusty grin spread across his face.

"So, Christianity has been in existence for two thousand years?" the second woman asked Joe. "I wish I could come with you to learn more, but I can't leave now. My contemplations sit on the edge of epiphany." She waved goodbye with a roll of her fingers, and gave Joe a smile that set his mind off in an unexpected direction. As she returned to the bush she appeared from, his eyes followed her curvaceous form until she disappeared.

The other woman leaned over to Joe and put her hands up and held his face. Joe made no effort stop her, gazing into her eyes. She sighed, and stroked his cheeks. He could see her drift away as he detailed the pure black of her pupils and the rich colour of the iris'. She drew closer to Joe, her breasts gently pressing against his shirt, he found he had no inclination or desire to pull away. She whispered, "Your skin is so wonderful to touch. So intricate. I wish to remove these robes, so we may press against each other and linger in those delightful sensations of flesh upon flesh. If you wish for me to come with you, I would surely change my mind in a moment and leave this place."

Joe's jaw dropped, his face flushed and his heart beat with a thrill that had been so long forgotten it felt new. He breathed in and caught her scent, and more, clear like the morning air.

She gazed into his eyes, and he was almost mesmerized.

He pulled away from her. "No, I'm sorry," he said. "Married you know."

"Truly?" asked the woman, looking disappointed.

"Yes," said Joe, more determined. This fantasy was clearly riddled with lustful thoughts. But the intensity of his arousal was many times greater than the night before, and he was uncomfortable with the feelings running through him.

She groaned gently and said, "You are so fresh." She sighed and turned back, allowing her hand to linger on Joe's face. As she disappeared into the bushes, he released the tension in his chest with a long breath.

Isaiah laughed. "How did you manage to refuse such a wondrous and beautiful woman?"

"It was not easy," breathed Joe, his hand holding his chest. "Anyway, apart from being married, it wouldn't do for a man of my age to be cavorting with someone as young as her."

"Young? Did you not hear? She's at least two thousand one hundred years older than you."

Joe laughed. "Not from where I'm standing."

"So I see," said Isaiah, pointing to the bulge in Joe's pants. Joe pulled his hat down, covering his crotch.

"Come Joe," said Isaiah still smiling. "Let's go, you can tell me all that you know of the current age. And the walk will calm your passions."

"Sure," said Joe. They started to walk back the way he had come. "What did the other lady whisper in your ear?"

"Why Joe, that's between me and the lady," said Isaiah. "And perhaps you've had enough excitement for one day."

Joe could not disagree.

Chapter 9

Isaiah was old. So old that Joe found it impossible to believe that anyone could be so old, and Isaiah had no idea how long he had been in the Fields of Solitude.

What threw Joe was when Isaiah said, "I've met this man Jesus."

"What?" said Joe.

"Yes. You spoke of Christianity. Started by a man called Jesus, was it not?"

"Apparently," said Joe.

"Apparently? You doubt it?"

"History is not clear on Jesus."

Isaiah laughed. "Indeed, history is not always a reliable teacher."

"But you think the Jesus you know is the same person?"

"I know he is. He lives in a house surrounded by pilgrims seeking his grace. Or he did. He may be gone, or the situation may have changed. In truth I did not expect the religion to last for so long as it did. But what do I know of such matters?"

Isaiah was sure of his acquaintance. During their walk Joe had told Isaiah all that he could. He was running out of answers for the inquisitive naked man, when they arrived at his house. How Joe had managed to make his way back was a mystery to him.

Isaiah was wonderstruck by the house even before they had entered it. Once Joe had opened the front door and shoved aside the fresh flyers, Isaiah walked in and inspected every aspect of the hallway. He ran his hands over the walls to feel how smooth they were. He looked closely into each and every corner, and cupboard. He searched through closets, the drawers in the kitchen wondering about the utensils and appliances, and eventually he saw the bottles of wine and sat down. Joe was about to say something, since Isaiah was still completely naked, but he was too slow.

"This wine is marvellous," said Isaiah, drinking it in gulps. "I haven't tasted wine in what must be hundreds of years. And these cups of crystal, so smoothly cut, what skill it must have taken to make these."

Then Joe heard the front door shut and he heard the footsteps in the corridor, and then Lilly's voice. "Joe are you there?" she shouted.

"In the living room," replied Joe. Then he remembered Isaiah was naked.

Lilly swept into the room, before Joe could say or do anything. "You are not going to fucking believe it," she started when she noticed Isaiah on the sofa. He immediately stood up, and Lilly gasped. He had an erection standing proud before him, and she tried desperately hard to avert her eyes.

"Hello," said Isaiah. "What a pleasure to meet you."

"The same I'm sure," she said, still looking everywhere but at him.

"Hey Isaiah, maybe you should get dressed," said Joe.

"Ah my nakedness offends you. I apologise," said Isaiah. He came forward to lean against the back of the sofa, hiding his manhood, and look more closely at Lilly. "But can you blame me with your shimmering hair, and such sparkling eyes?" he said, in warm tones. Lilly appeared confused by Isaiah's manner, and was flattered. He looked at Joe. "Though first I must have some clothing."

"Of course," said Joe. "You can take some from one of the other rooms." He led Isaiah upstairs.

"By the stars," said Isaiah, once they were out of the living room and climbing the stairs. "You share this house with that beauty? You are a lucky man."

Joe squirmed. "I think you might be assuming too much," he said.

Isaiah laughed. "So, you have no interest in her?"

"No."

"Then let me take one of these rooms."

"You want to stay here?" asked Joe. "Just because of Lilly? Who looks like she could be your grandmother?

"Yes. That and I have no place," said Isaiah. "I have no recollection of the home I lived in so long ago. I have wandered and slept under stars, in the rain and snow. So let me stay here with you and I can learn more of the modern age."

Joe thought for a moment, and then shrugged. "I have no problem with it. Not like I paid for this house, or anything else."

"Good," smiled Isaiah and went to find a bedroom.

"Not that one or that one," said Joe pointing.

"Which of the two is yours?"

Joe pointed at his door. Isaiah chose the room opposite Lilly's.

Lilly was in the living room drinking the wine Isaiah had opened, when Joe went back down.

"He's a little unusual," said Joe. "But a good chap. Does seem very... randy."

"You're not kidding. Where did you meet him?"

"In the Fields of Solitude."

"The what?!"

"The Fields of Solitude," repeated Joe. "Though they didn't appear to be very solitary. Seemed to be lots of people about."

"I'm sure he'll tell me more when he comes back," said Lilly. "But I want to tell you before I forget. Your son was wonderful."

Joe was immediately interested in listening to Lilly. "Really?" he asked.

"Yeah, very thoughtful. Unlike his father." Joe was momentarily annoyed, but didn't say anything. Lilly carried on any way and went into great details of the day. She was obviously emotional, since it was her funeral. She felt that Willow had done an excellent job of organising it. Understandably it had to be a closed casket, and whatever could be gathered up of Lilly's body was cremated. Willow had gone through Lilly's old contacts, and some of Lilly's travelling friends had even made it. The ceremony was simple, and it was a buffet, but everything was tasteful.

Sam had delivered the note from Deb with some words that Lilly had told them he should say. Sam delivered the words with great care, and Willow read the note to Joseph and Cloud, when they were alone after the ceremony and reception of course. She didn't tell Joe what the message was, but she said it was the best she could do, and her family were surprised by it. After Samuel left, she saw the smile returning to her daughter's face. Then she stopped talking suddenly and paused to dwell on the moment.

Joe reached out a hand and put it on Lilly's. She was surprised by his sudden familiarity. "I'm happy for you," he said. "I remember how good it was to see my family."

Lilly looked like she was about to say something, but then changed her mind. Joe pulled his hand away when he heard Isaiah enter the room.

"Tell me, what do you think?" asked Isaiah, holding out his arms. He began a turn in his bright multi-coloured and patterned beach shirt, and green shorts. He had shaven his beard.

When he finished his turn, the smile was still on his face and he looked at Lilly and Joe for comment.

"That's bright," said Joe.

"Oh yeah, everyone's going to notice you," said Lilly.

"As they should," declared Isaiah. He was clearly pleased with himself. "I have never known cloth with a cut this comfortable before. Only the finest silks could compare."

Joe laughed. "Come and sit down," he said. "We'll drink some more wine and we can watch a movie."

"What's a movie?" asked Isaiah sitting down next to Lilly. Lilly moved over to give herself space.

Joe smiled. "Let me pour you a drink and you'll see," he said.

"Hey, you know what?" said Lilly. "This is a perfect time for a doob." She pulled out a joint.

Chapter 10

They had consumed more bottles of wine whilst they had watched the movie, and Isaiah was amazed. He asked numerous questions about the story. When did it happen, and could he meet the actress? Joe and Lilly explained that it was like a recording of theater. Isaiah called it magic. Then he said, "Like the magic of the sky people." Joe's ears pricked up immediately.

"The sky people?" asked Joe.

"Yes," said Isaiah. "They had the most incredible powers. They came out of the sky in metal birds and met with us."

"You mean aliens?" asked Joe.

"What do you mean aliens?" asked Isaiah. "They came from the sky. Their home was among the stars."

Joe started to laugh. "Ok," he scoffed. "Now I know I'm definitely dreaming."

"What do you mean?" asked Isaiah annoyed by Joe's tone.

"There are no sky people," said Joe. "No aliens. That's a ridiculous idea."

"Do you call me a liar?" Isaiah was outraged. He

stood up and faced Joe. Despite the attire he was still intimidating.

"Now hold on," said Joe. "There's no need to get upset."

"You call me a liar. How dare you!" said Isaiah. "I saw them fly down to the ground in giant metal birds. The sides of the birds would open and they would come out wearing clothing covering their entire bodies, made of fine threads of silver and gold. They told us they had travelled from distant worlds."

Joe was dumb struck. Isaiah was passionate and certain of what he saw. "And around their heads were domes of crystal, with rings of light."

"Wow," said Lilly. "That reminds me of a documentary I saw on TV."

Joe stood up. He faced Isaiah and he looked at Lilly. He took a breath, and said, "Alright. So where are they?"

"Where are they?" repeated Isaiah.

"Yeah," said Joe. "Where are they?"

"I shall take you to some," said Isaiah.

"Oh really?"

"And when you meet them, you will apologise for your doubt."

"You were probably hallucinating."

"What do you mean?"

"You must have done some of those ancient drugs. Seeing things. Did this happen during some kind of pagan ceremony?"

"Ignorant fool. You think you know so much? I

will not dally words with you, I shall do. You will follow me."

Isaiah turned to leave.

"You know it's the middle of the night?" said Joe. "And I'm drunk!"

Isaiah looked at the windows, and turned back. "We will go in the morning," he said. "I too am drunk."

"Good idea," said Joe. "I'll see you in the morning."

They both turned and went to their rooms. Lilly muttered, "Wow," and picked up what was left of a joint from the ashtray.

Chapter 11

Isaiah was already in the kitchen eating fruit form the bowl on the breakfast bar, when Joe came down. Joe remembered the fruit he had eaten with Lilly on the first night and helped himself to an apple. Its sweet juices washed down his throat and he felt the moisture in his chest.

"So good," said Joe.

"Mmm," said Isaiah.

"Did you sleep well?"

"The bed is amazing," said Isaiah. "It was firm, and the sheets were soft. Such luxuries were always for kings and emperors."

"Would you like some coffee?" asked Joe.

Isaiah looked at Joe curiously, "Coffee?" he asked. "I always like coffee."

Minutes later Joe and Isaiah were savouring the aroma of freshly ground coffee.

"Nice?" asked Joe, smiling with satisfaction.

"Very interesting," said Isaiah.

Joe gave a cup to Isaiah and took a sip. "Oh yeah," he sighed.

Isaiah sipped the coffee. "By the holiest of holies," he said, looking at the hot liquid in the cup. He took another mouthful and then another, until the cup was empty, in the time Joe took another sip. "I had forgotten how wonderful it was."

"Would you like some more?" asked Joe.

"Oh yes," said Isaiah.

"Make one for me too." It was Lilly shouting from the living room.

Joe was shocked to hear her voice. "How long have you been there?" he shouted back, through the dining room.

"All night," said Lilly. "I fell asleep on the sofa."

Lilly walked the length of the dining room and, as she walked, Joe looked more closely at her. To his surprise she was not as bedraggled as he expected her to be. She had drunk and smoked as much as him if not more and did not have hair that was ruffled too much, nor skin that was off colour, and he could not be sure but he felt her hair was not as white as he remembered. "Are you hungover?" he asked.

Lilly thought and was herself surprised to say, "No." Then she added. "But I should be. I lost track about half way through a bottle and I remember feeling seriously uneasy. After a night like that I should feel like shit. You?"

"No." The realisation also surprised Joe.

"A benefit of the afterlife," said Isaiah.

"Maybe," said Joe.

"Not that again," said Lilly. "I don't feel terrible, but I do feel a little fuzzy. Hurry up with that coffee."

Joining Isaiah and Joe at the breakfast table, "So," said Lilly to Isaiah, with a twinkle in her eye. "We're going to see aliens today. I've got to admit, I'm feeling a little excited," she giggled. Isaiah was very pleased and smiling, leaned in a little closer to Lilly. Lilly, smiling sweetly, gently backed away.

Joe gave Lilly the cup of coffee and they enjoyed the drink in silence. When they were done Isaiah stood up and announced, "It's a beautiful day, it will be a good walk." He had found classically styled sunglasses with a red wire rim and was already wearing leather sandals. Joe wondered about the footwear, it was in contrast to the bright green knee length shorts and the yellow shirt, that appeared to have its own illumination. Joe wondered about the clothes. He had avoided all the colourful clothes in his cupboard, but it was a vast cupboard. Given the variety of footwear he had, he knew he must have sandals somewhere in his room.

"I think I'd like to wear my sunglasses too," said Joe and went back to his room. He returned ready to go having selected walking shoes from the hallway cloakroom. Lilly was also prepared to go. She had chosen a wide brimmed straw hat, and it served to remind Joe to get his own hat.

Isaiah led them out of the house.

"Oh lord, what is this?" asked Isaiah, as soon as

they had left the house. "The colours are brightened, and they're so clear. And yet the light has also been reduced so my eyes are less troubled." He pulled off the sunglasses and looked more closely at them.

"Sounds like they're polarised," said Joe.

Joe put on his own sunglasses and was amazed at what he saw. He was looking at more than polarized light. He was seeing beyond anything he could describe in words. It was like light as he expected to see it, with additional layers that added to the sight he was born with.

"Polarised? Tell me what does polarised mean?"

For the first time in years Joe had an enthusiastic listener. Isaiah paid close attention to everything Joe said and questioned him to the point of having to explain the derivation of some theories. As they walked Joe recalled all those seminal lessons and lectures that had led to his position as an academic. All this whilst Joe was trying to adjust to the enhanced view he was getting through his own glasses.

"This is a fascinating science lesson," commented Lilly. "You should get to the part where you tell him he's just a figment of your imagination, and none of this is real."

"What? You think you're in a dream?" asked Isaiah.

Joe did not answer immediately. "It's hard to take in," said Joe. "Look at what I'm doing. Walking. I'm supposed to be in the afterlife, and I'm walking to meet aliens. I thought I would meet God. I thought I would meet passed friends and family. I've met my still living family, through my clairvoyant cousin Deb, and seen Lilly's family. I actually went to my own Shiva, apart from that no one else. I did meet some wolves. And you."

"Wolves," noted Isaiah. "Interesting."

"It was," said Joe. "Quite a profound experience."

"A profound experience in your own mind," said Isaiah, laughing.

"I wish I could meet those relatives who died before me. I really thought I would, if there was an afterlife."

"So did I," said Isaiah.

"Oh yeah?"

"However, I don't believe I have," said Isaiah. "Though so many years have passed since my death, where would I begin to look for them now?" he laughed.

"I'd like to meet my wife," said Joe.

"Why?" asked Isaiah.

"Why? Because I miss her, and I want to see her again. If I'm really dead, why isn't she here? We loved each other."

"If this is your fantasy, then only you can answer that."

"Oh come on," said Joe. "How many people have control of their own sub-conscious? We barely understand how the human mind works."

"What is the sub-conscious?"

"Now you're asking," laughed Lilly.

Joe was at a loss as to how to explain the sub-conscious. He knew he wasn't doing very well when, after a considerable length of time, Isaiah asked. "So you're saying there's more than one person within me?"

"No. There's only you."

"From your words I'm led to believe there are many within me, and I am not in control of myself. It would seem you're suggesting I may be possessed."

"You are not possessed!"

Whilst Isaiah ruminated, Lilly leaned over to Joe and whispered, "Not going so great?"

"It's a tricky subject, and not one I'm familiar with."

"You don't say."

Isaiah turned to Joe. "I have seen a man possessed," he said.

"How do you know he was possessed?" asked Joe.

"It was obvious from the manner of his shaking and gesticulations. He had the strength of ten men, and in his eyes could be seen the madness of a beast. He killed many of my men before we were able to subdue him."

"So, what did you do?"

"We bound him and the priest battled the beast within."

"How did he do that?"

"With sacred songs and symbols, potions and the power of his own belief."

Joe did his best to keep the scorn from his voice. "Did that work?"

Isaiah looked at Joe. "You may mock as you like,

but faith offers a power that transcends the limits of men."

"What happened to the man?"

"He died. The demon took his soul."

"That's unfortunate," said Joe.

"Yes," said Isaiah. "He was a good fighter."

Isaiah led them up the mountain to the clouds, and Joe became enchanted by what he saw from the high slopes. They stopped to look about and sat on boulders to appreciate all that was around them. The glasses enhanced everything that he saw, from the striations in the rocks to the glimmer of the clouds. Joe had no idea how long it was before they resumed their journey, but they did not rush. Lilly lit another of Dan's spliffs.

Satisfied with their break, they went higher above the clouds. When they passed through them again, the clouds changed slowly into an atmosphere that was more liquid than gas.

Then they were standing on rock that was far below the surface of an ocean. The plant life changed and was many coloured. With the glasses the colours appeared on multiple levels. They spotted strange creatures curiously swimming by them, or hiding behind rocks. When they looked up, Joe saw the shimmer like being under water, but this liquid was less dense than water. Moving about was easy, but the liquid would not have supported him if he tried to swim. Joe did not know if it was night or day, but the stars were easily visible shining through the surface.

Their visual senses were overwhelmed and Joe and Isaiah took off their sunglasses.

"By god," said Isaiah. "This is amazing. It's nothing like the world I saw the last time I made the journey."

"What happened last time?" asked Joe.

"Ah," said Isaiah. "I saw the forefathers of the sky people. They are long lived and may still be living even in your age. I wish I could meet those that came to us. What powers they possessed. How they cherished us."

"Like gods?" asked Joe.

"Some of my tribes said as such, but they did not claim to be so. However, I must admit, there were many of them who were pleased by the worship, those that adored them were well rewarded."

Isaiah looked up, "They're coming," he said.

"Welcome." The greeting was in Joe's head. He was shocked and looked around, since there was no one to be seen.

"Where are they?" asked Joe. "I can't see them."

"As I said, they are coming," said Isaiah. "Did you hear them?"

"Yes, I did," said Joe. "Right in my head!"

"Holy fuck," said Lilly. "Is that telepathy?"

"I don't care what it was!" said Joe. "They were in my head!"

"You do not like their way of communicating?"

"No I do not! Not in my head!"

"But if it's not real, what does it matter?" asked Isaiah. "It's just you in your own mind."

Joe grimaced, and turned back to wait for the aliens. Their forms approached in the distance, like missiles they flew through the liquid atmosphere. They were spread out coming from all directions, and once they were close great sail-like fins swept out to stop them so they floated suspended around the visitors. As they crowded around, there was no gap between them that Joe could see.

Each of the aliens had three eyes. One eye at the top and the other two evenly spaced to the sides around a central snout. There were various types of protrusions around the base of the snout, and Joe guessed that they were sensors. Just by their mouths were two tentacles. There were two large fins on top and smaller ones below, and behind them were larger tentacles that were swept back and Joe could just make them out. What was particularly impressive about the aliens was the incredible myriad of colours of each individual, constantly changing. No one was the same.

Joe did not hear anything more in his mind but Isaiah spoke in response to them. "It's good to meet you," he said. "I've never met your kind before." Isaiah turned to Joe and Lilly, and said to them, "They're called the Hoola." Joe instinctively raised a hand and waved.

One of the aliens quickly shot out a tentacle and touched Joe's waving hand. He snatched his hand back and it snatched back the tentacle. Then Joe paused, and looked at his hand, and reflecting on how the alien skin felt. Nothing like he could ever have expected. A thrill ran through him, and the alien shimmered, and the colours of its skin changed rapidly as the surface trembled gently. It slowly settled down again. A series of clicks and hoots emanated from the creature and Joe instinctively said, "It's alright. I don't mind."

Any tension Joe felt immediately disappeared. He couldn't get over the sensation of touching the creature. Isaiah spoke to them for a while, and then Joe noticed Isaiah put his sunglasses back and laugh saying, "That's even more amazing."

"What is it?" asked Joe.

"See for yourself," said Isaiah.

Joe put on his sunglasses and immediately saw the greater contrasts and the range of other colours that he would never have seen otherwise. He was silenced once again.

"What?" said Lilly. "What do you see?"

"They can talk to me," said Joe to Isaiah. Then he spoke directly to the aliens. "You can talk to me."

"For fuck's sake, Joe, what do you see?" asked Lilly.

Joe took off the sunglasses and gave them to Lilly. "Try these," he said. She put them on and stood gaping at the aliens.

"I should have found a pair too," muttered Lilly. "This is better than acid."

"Yeah," said Joe. "Now give them back."

"In a minute," said Lilly, waving Joe away.

"Hey they're my glasses," objected Joe.

Joe forgot the sunglasses as his mind immediately

started to hear the chatter from the Hoola, and it was full of so much more than mere words could convey. Their sense of excitement filled every thought they shared, and they were most excited and thrilled that life went on past their deaths. Meeting Joe, Lilly and Isaiah was one of the most amazing things that their race could hope for.

The three companions found places to sit, and exchanged thoughts with the Hoola.

"Aliens," said the Hoola excitedly. "Life on other worlds. The questions we have asked, which are unravelled in death. An end that is not an end." The aliens all sparkled with rolling colours appearing in different patterns on each of them. Joe sensed the joy they were feeling at the new adventure.

All three of the visitors had many questions as well. Joe listened as the Hoola explained their history, which was easily and quickly relayed to the three companions. In the aliens' excitement too quickly at times, the companions barely kept up.

The Hoola had gained telepathy in the recent past, an event called the Mystic Change. Before the change they were at a basic level in their evolution. They were still living in small groups and building homes from the rocks and mud, and wondering what was above the great ocean when the change came. The change did not come slowly and steadily as one might expect, but swept across their world within a generation. It was a giant evolutionary leap.

The Hoola appeared to have taken the change as

easily as they swam through the ocean. Somehow they had felt no fear at the new ability, but felt liberated and began to question and think in new ways.

It was not long after the emergence of the telepathy that the world of the Hoola began to change as well. Small communities became larger, and infrastructure started to appear. Their development was rapid, despite numerous setbacks. It was obvious that the Hoolas' need to understand and discover was a powerful driver. They had many accidents and took enormous risks, and they all felt the terrible loss of life, but they continued taking chances with new ideas. To an outsider they might have appeared callous, in their pursuit of knowledge.

None of the aliens had believed in an afterlife. That was obvious from their history. Once the telepathy was in every one of them, they found that they had no more answers than before, but were able to debate more intensely. The dominant conclusion was that without the proof then life was finite. They had all accepted that they would live and then die, and did not believe in anything they could not perceive.

In their explanations Joe realized that one of the greatest mysteries they had was how they had achieved telepathy. They had tried to explain how it worked and carried out a host of tests, but the ability remained elusive. Their researches were not without worth, they helped them to understand and improve their use of the amazing ability, which led to benefits in other areas of their lives. None the less, Joe did sense frustration at their inability to discover why the telepathy had manifested.

When Joe asked them why they were so ready to believe they were in an afterlife, they told him they did not question the existence of an afterlife since they were in it, and they trusted their senses. Then they asked him, "In your history you have religion, and many believe there is life beyond death. From our discussions, it is fair to say that a greater majority of your world believe this. Why do you doubt this belief? Why do you feel you are in a dream? Even now you wonder why your subconscious would show you us."

Joe explained in the best way he could, and because of the telepathy, the Hoola were able to understand. They did not press the subject any further, and returned to their sciences, and the telling of the litany of catastrophes that preceded every great achievement.

They had discovered explosives when one of the Hoola had learnt from another about the properties of certain substances when combined with others. That Hoola had then found a method of speeding up the reaction, creating their first chemical explosion. The Hoola had blown itself up in the process, but not before he had detailed his experiment and recorded it. There was a statue erected to the Hoola who discovered the chemical reaction. One thing the Hoola liked to do was commemorate their dead, with great care and affection. Joe wished he could pronounce the name of the scientist, or any of the Hoola's names, but they went beyond words.

Images of the Hoola's landscape appeared from their memories. The raw features of their world were all around them, but they had built cities and those were the images Joe and his companions saw. There were memorials throughout their cities. So much so that the city authorities passed laws to designate special places for the memorials since they were starting to get in the way.

Then the Hoola who were talking to them fell silent, and appeared to bow. A gap opened and they made way for a single one of their kind. It was about fifty percent larger than the others, and another obvious difference were the fins, which were shaped differently to cover more of the body. The body was slightly longer. It did not rush but swam serenely around the three humans. Joe turned to Isaiah and asked, "What's going on?" Isaiah shrugged.

Lilly laughed. "Yep," she said. "They're real fucking dumb sometimes." A series of clicks and hoots came from the new Hoola. "Ok," said Lilly. "Good to meet you too."

The large Hoola then calmly swam away through the gap made by the others. Once it was gone the others turned back.

"What was that?" asked Joe.

"That was one of their women," answered Lilly excited. "They fucking rule here."

Lilly pulled out a joint. "I wonder if I could light it in this... What is it? Water?" she asked.

"Definitely not water," said Joe.

Lilly shrugged, took out a lighter and was pleased to be able to light the joint. "Oh yeah," she sighed, reclining on the rocks and losing herself in the visual display of the Hoola and their world.

"How many of those have you got?" asked Joe.

"Dan and I rolled a few. You know, for later."

The Hoola sensed the change in Lilly's mind and their curiosity was piqued. They gathered around her, fascinated by what Lilly was doing and experiencing. Joe and Isaiah relaxed with Lilly and when the joint was finished Joe found that he needed to go back. The world of the Hoola was profoundly different in so many ways, not just with the environment, but also with the culture of the aliens. They felt his need to leave and understood. He looked to Lilly and Isaiah.

"Are you guys ready to go?" asked Joe.

"I'm ready," said Lilly.

"Yes," said Isaiah.

Then one of the aliens came forward and Joe understood that he had been dead for some time longer than his friends. "We have a request," said the Hoola. "May one of us travel with you? It seems death allows us to transcend the limitations that kept us so far apart. We have not yet encountered your species, and we desire knowledge of your people and customs."

Joe, Lilly and Isaiah smiled. "Of course," they said.

The aliens shimmered with excitement. "Wow!"

grinned Lilly. Joe wondered if he made a lunge for the sunglasses, would he be able to get them from her. The Hoola sensed his thought, and an excited flicker went across them, followed by a disappointed dimming when Joe decided he was too old for that nonsense and strode off. He became annoyed as, on the walk back, Lilly continually enthused about everything she saw.

Chapter 12

To say that the visit to the Hoola had a profound or dramatic effect on Joe would have been an understatement.

The alien who had joined them was happily swimming through the air among the trees, despite the lack of the liquid from which he had come. He commented on the trees and other foliage. Joe had noticed all the vegetation that had been around him when he was on the Hoola's world, if it was all vegetation. He also noticed the variety of creatures that were swimming around, but had not given them any thought. All his attention had gone on the intelligent creatures that were communicating with him.

Joe completely ignored the impossibility of the Hoola's ability to swim in air, given he was aware of how much denser the fluid the Hoola lived in was. Or that he had somehow breathed the liquid as well. The transition from the air to the fluid of the Hoola's world was so gentle he had been unaware of the change, and when he was, he had noticed how he could feel the fluid flowing into his lungs. He could barely describe the sensation, but it was not one he would forget quickly.

When they got back to the house the alien flew around enquiring about everything they did. Joe went to his room to take a moment, but it didn't help. The sensations he was feeling were still strong, and defied his belief.

There was a wallet in Joe's pocket that he had not opened since he had woken up in this place. He left it alone and went downstairs. He found everyone at the back of the house.

Lilly was thrilled to have the Hoola with them, and she ran through the trees like she was twenty years younger. In fact, when Joe looked at her, he noticed how the amount of grey in her hair was diminished, and how her skin appeared to have tightened over her face, and the firmness that was appearing through the clothing. There was no doubt she was getting younger.

Isaiah was relaxing on a sunbed and Joe looked at the bottle of beer that Isaiah was enjoying. "One minute," he said. He went into the house and came back out with a cold beer and pulled up a garden chair. He twisted the top off and raised the bottle. They clinked bottles and drank.

"Damn that's good beer," said Joe.

"Indeed" said Isaiah happily. He looked at the bottle. "How much the world has changed," he said.

"You seem to be at ease with the modern world. You ask questions but have no trouble adjusting."

Isaiah held up the reefer. "I used to smoke this

from clay pipes. Now there is paper so thin, and with a sticky edge, and the effect it offers is so different to the pipe. But in both ages the aim was to burn the flowers and breath in the smoke." He took another draw on the joint. "I was too long in the Fields of Solitude."

Joe laughed. "You spent centuries being wound up by a dead parrot," he said.

Isaiah laughed wistfully, "That parrot was full of pranks. He gave me company when I needed it."

"Do you really have no idea how long you were in the Fields of Solitude?"

"None. After a while time becomes irrelevant."

"How did you avoid other people? Seemed to me like you were always within shouting distance from the next person."

Isaiah laughed. "That is a mystery to me too," said Isaiah. "Can you accept that we simply did?"

Joe laughed as well. "I guess I have to," he said.

"What's funny?" asked Lilly approaching from among the trees. She took the joint from Isaiah. She forgot her question, distracted by the alien bobbing about around her, watching her take the smoke.

"He did the same with me," said Isaiah.

When Lilly drew the smoke and let out a plume before inhaling, the alien nipped in close and sucked in the stray cloud, making Lilly giggle.

Joe sensed the effect of the smoke in the Hoola, as its spectrum of colours slowed from a rapid excited cycle to a slow and mellow rhythm. "What should we call you," he asked. The alien expressed his name with a series of sounds and thought.

"We've been trying that," said Joe. "Quite frankly it just sounds, and feels stupid when we do it."

"This is true," said Isaiah.

The alien laughed, in a gently high-pitched trill. "It does sound ridiculous," he said.

"How about we call you a name that we can say?"

The alien assented to Joe's request. Lilly, Joe and Isaiah fell silent as they stared at the trees trying to think of an appropriate name, whilst the alien's senses moved back and forth between them, in anticipation.

As the excitement grew in the Hoola, Lilly had an idea, "I know," she said. "How about Kal, like in kaleidoscope."

"Of course," said Joe looking at Kal.

"What's a kaleidoscope?" asked Isaiah.

Kal was delighted with his new name. He opened his fins and shimmered, appearing like a kaleidoscope. He conveyed the meaning to Isaiah.

They sensed Kal's amusement. Joe wondered about the new form of communication that was being revealed to him. He only shared it with Kal, as they all did. He wondered what it would be like to share the connection with Isaiah, or Lilly. He immediately ended the line of thought.

"Tell me," said Joe. "What part of our lives would you like to experience first?"

Kal thought for a moment. "Food," he said. "I would like to try your food."

"I think we can do something about that," said Joe. He decided it would not be a good idea to offer to cook, instead he walked back to the house and returned with a pile of the flyers from the front door.

Spreading the flyers on the garden table they gathered round to see the options. There were many choices that Joe had never heard of before, but it was Lilly who became most excited.

"What's pizza?" asked Isaiah.

Kal was also curious, and Lilly had a look of disbelief. She said to Isaiah "Kal I understand, but you must surely have heard of Pizza?"

"When did it come about? There is much that has passed since my isolation."

"Pizza's old. It must be as old as the Romans," said Lilly.

Isaiah looked at the menu. "These pictures suggest it's bread with pieces of vegetables and meats on top," he said. "It does not seem so special, but the detail of these images and the brightness of the colours, they make pizza very appealing."

"Listen," said Lilly. "If the rest of the food we've had is anything to go by, I want pizza," she finished emphasizing a deep desire.

Joe laughed, "Well why not?" he said. "We have the Assyrian Cook House with food from thousands of years ago and god knows what else."

"Don't worry," said Isaiah. "That Assyrian food is not so wondrous as it appears, and it lacks character. Like it's people."

"I thought it was all great in the afterlife," said Joe.

"Have faith," said Isaiah. "No aspect of it gave me hope for the Assyrians, it's not worth trying." He got up. "Come, let's try pizza."

"Well alright," said Joe. "I don't know how to get there. Do you know where we should go?"

"Of course," said Isaiah. "I shall hold this colourful parchment and with it we shall find our destination." Putting on his sunglasses, Isaiah led the way out of the house and along a trail through the trees, with Kal gliding through the air beside him, looking confident with his direction.

Joe turned to Lilly and whispered to her, "Why do you think he hates the Assyrians so much?"

"I don't even know who the Assyrians are," said Lilly.

"The Assyrian Empire was around about 1400 BC."

"Oh, thank god," said Lilly. "I thought I was being dumb."

Joe looked at Lilly quizzically. "Not knowing something doesn't make you dumb," he said.

Lilly smiled a little. "You were saying," she said.

"My point is that was a long time ago. Thousands of years long ago."

"Shit yeah. That is a long time. Definitely a long time to bear a grudge."

They walked on for a little longer and the air became dryer than the atmosphere of the forest where Joe and Lilly were living. The track had become dusty and as they cleared a group of trees, it led to stone houses of varying sizes. In the distance Joe could see a sign for Shin and Ru's Pizza Place.

When they got to Shin and Ru's, Joe estimated it to be about midday, and they were surprised to see a queue. A little further down the street there were other restaurants and there were queues outside them as well.

There was a steady stream of people coming out of the restaurant carrying pizzas as others were going in. Two long haired and heavily bearded hippies, were stood in front of Joe and his friends. They were hippies to Joe's mind since they were wearing tie-dyed shirts and trousers cut off above the ankle and sandals. Joe casually asked, "Been waiting long?"

"No man," said the first of the hippies. "Shin just went for a break, and Ru can just about keep up with demand."

"What do you mean?" asked Joe. The hippy pointed behind Joe and when he turned around, he was surprised to see the large number of people who had appeared behind them. The queue now extended at least fifty feet down the dirt track that was the road.

"I didn't even see them arrive," said Joe.

The queue was moving steadily though more people were arriving than were leaving.

"This place is popular," said Lilly.

"Food must be good," said Isaiah.

"Best pizza around," said one of the hippies.

"It's the only pizza place around man," said the other hippy, laughing.

Kal floated down to join Joe and the others, and a shout came out from the line behind. "No cutting in!"

"He's not cutting in," shouted Lilly. "He's with us." Adding, "Fucking queue Nazi."

"I heard that," came the shout from the objector.

Lilly quickly turned around. "So what're you going to do about it?"

The objector waved away Lilly and turned back to her friends.

"Calm down, Lilly," said Joe.

"Why?" said Lilly, "I can say whatever I fucking like."

"That doesn't mean you have to be obnoxious."

"Obnoxious?" said Lilly. "You're calling me obnoxious?"

Joe looked around nervously. "Alright, I'm sorry for calling you obnoxious."

Lilly wasn't done. "Am I embarrassing you Joe?"

"You are when you shout like that,' said Joe, glaring at her.

"Oh yeah?" Lilly glared back at Joe.

"Yeah!"

As Lilly and Joe argued a man in front of them in the queue, turned to the group. "Hey," he said, looking around. "You want really good pizza?"

"That's why we're here," said Lilly.

The stranger pulled out a flyer from inside his shirt and handed it to Joe, whilst continuing to check his surroundings. Lilly, Isaiah and Kal looked over Joe's shoulder. The flyer was advertising another pizza restaurant, with a banner claiming it was the best.

"This place is shit," said the stranger. "You want real pizza you go to an Italian place. Like Coccini's." He pointed at the name on the flyer.

He quickly moved on to the people behind Joe's group.

"Should we go there?" asked Kal.

"Why?" said Isaiah.

"The man stated this place was shit. He claims this place, Coccini's, is better."

"Did you not sense any dishonesty from him?"

Kal paused before replying. "No."

"He was merely trying to lessen the popularity of this place by redirecting the patrons to his inn. The man is likely a liar, and therefore not to be trusted."

"How do you know he was lying? Perhaps this place is shit and his is better."

Kal had further questions, and Isaiah was happy to explain.

"Dude is this alien with you?" asked the first hippy. The two of them were fascinated by Kal and appeared not to be able to look away.

"Wow, he is amazing," said the second hippy.

Another shout came from further back in the queue. "Hey arsehole, want to get a move on?"

Lilly shouted back, "What's the matter with you shithead? You starving or something?"

There was a shout from further back in the queue. "Hey Angelo, what the fuck are you doing here?"

"What's your problem?" said Angelo.

"What do you think arsehole? You trying to steal our patrons again?"

"Not stealing, just informing them?"

"Of what? How shit your pizzas are?"

"Hey fuck you, Shin. Our pizzas are the best. Made the authentic way by real Italians."

"Times change. Food evolves, gets better. That's why you're so backward."

"With that dough mix? That's not pizza dough. You're fooling these good people."

The argument went from an exchange of insults to the point when Angelo and Shin were within nose to nose. "Well come on Angelo, let's see what you've got."

A dark suited being appeared. "Hello boys," he said. "What seems to be the problem?"

Angelo and Shin immediately backed away from one another. "Nothing," said Angelo.

"We were just discussing the finer points of pizza dough. That's all," said Shin.

"That's good to know," said the dark one. "Don't you have diners waiting for you Angelo?"

"Oh yeah," said Angelo. "Yeah, I better get back to them."

"Yeah, fuck off Angelo," said Shin.

Angelo left walking down the line and passing out the flyers as he went.

"Lots of diners here too, Shin."

Shin strode to the restaurant. The dark suited man

walked away from the queue and inexplicably disappeared.

Joe looked past the two hippies and noticed the queue had moved on. "Pay attention guys. The people in front are up to the door."

"What?" said the second hippy. He turned around to see the back of the queue. Then he looked up at the sign. "Shit man, we're at Shin and Ru's."

"Want to move on guys?" asked Joe.

They watched the two hippies patiently as they realised what they were doing. The first hippy turned around to them and said, "Oh yeah, we came out for pizza." They moved quickly to the doors and went inside.

Inside the restaurant, the design looked like something from the fifties. The music was from the time, as were the decorations, with sculptures and pictures.

The two hippies stared at the menu on the board above the counter. The aromas of the pizzas and their ingredients wafted over from the ovens, and Joe started salivating and looked at the menu with greater personal interest.

"Hey guys," said the attendant behind the counter. "What do you want?"

"Give us a minute man, I'm just having trouble with your colours," said the second hippy.

"Yeah man, those colours are wild," said the first.

The attendant smiled. "What did you do today guys?" she asked. "Mushrooms again?" The hippies nodded and smiled.

Joe looked at the board and had to admit the menu was colourful and under the right influence, could be very confusing.

Joe was curious. "Are mushrooms like acid?" he asked.

"Kinda," said the first hippy. "You want some? We found them in a field over that way." He pointed in a direction. The second hippy said, "No man, don't listen to him. They're over that way," and pointed in a completely different direction.

"Hey guys," came a shout from further back. "Hurry up."

"What? You gotta be somewhere?" shouted Lilly.

The person who had shouted waved Lilly away.

"Lilly," pleaded Joe. "Come on."

"Alright," said Lilly. "I just find that annoying."

The two hippies had paused to watch the drama, the woman behind the counter tried again. "So guys, have you decided or should I just get you your usual?"

"That would be great, Mika," said the first hippy.

"Alright," smiled Mika. "Why don't you go and sit down and I'll bring it over when it's ready."

"Thanks Mika," said the hippies, and they wandered to an empty table by the windows sat down and stared at the world outside.

"So guys," said Mika to Joe and his group. "What would you like?"

"Margherita," said Lilly without hesitation.

"I'll have the same," said Joe.

Isaiah had been looking at the pizzas the other

patrons were already eating and followed Joe and Lilly with the Margherita pizza. Kal being ignorant of what a Margherita pizza was, simply went along with the others.

A table became available and Isaiah and Kal went over to it. Before joining them, Lilly turned to Joe and said, "Sorry about getting angry in the queue." Joe was surprised. He had not expected any kind of apology from Lilly. "You're surprised?" asked Lilly. Joe shrugged, not quite sure how to answer. "I suppose you should be, and you're right. I'm not the apologetic type. But I've been thinking about my life and it's amazing how clearly I remember it. How much of it plays out in my mind, and just pops in there when I'm really not expecting it. There's so much stuff that I just pushed aside and forgot."

Lilly looked down at her hands, with her fingers interlocked in a firm grip. She was fighting tears and Joe instinctively reached out and put his hand over hers. "It's alright," he said. "I shouldn't be embarrassed. I have no right to judge you or tell you how you should behave."

The tension in her eased, and she smiled at Joe.

"I was just thinking about the free food. Thinking about how many times I struggled when I was younger, and the people that helped me." She laughed. "Course, there're the people that screwed me too. Figuratively and literally."

Before Joe could say anything else, Kal and Isaiah called them over, a chef was at the table with their order. Lilly pulled herself together and they went over to the table.

"How are you guys," asked the chef. "I've got four Margherita pizzas for you."

The chef put the pizzas on the table and asked if they wanted any drinks. The choice of drinks was extensive, and Joe settled on a juice.

"So how long have you been dead?" asked the chef.

Isaiah had lost track of time, and Joe and Lilly guessed they had been dead for a couple of months, but Lilly was pretty sure that was completely wrong. "Well, I'm Ru," said the chef. They introduced themselves and for some reason they were then talking about the latest things that Joe and Lilly could remember, and it seemed as if they had a lot to tell. The chef went and came back a couple of times before they had finished their pizzas and had to leave. The eating of the pizza was a leisurely experience, the conversation taking longer than the actual eating. They had no idea how long they had been there when they left.

Kal also enjoyed the food. He had not expected the flavours he got, and asked how the bread was made, then where the flour came from. Ru was very knowledgeable and happily explained all that she could, in between cooking and helping to serve the other patrons.

"My flour comes from that guy," said Ru, pointing at a man staring and inspecting the reactions of the patrons to the food they were eating. Occasionally he approached the diners and asked them questions.

"What's he doing?" asked Lilly.

"He's checking how the dough turned out. He was in the kitchen earlier to see how we mixed the flour."

"Seriously?" asked Joe.

"Oh yeah, he's a perfectionist."

On the way home Kal had many more questions.

"Don't rush," said Isaiah. "You have all the time you could want to gather knowledge."

Kal appeared to take Isaiah's advice, but there was nothing that could diminish his enthusiasm. Leaving the subject of the pizza, he asked about the mushrooms. He conversed with Lilly for the rest of the walk.

Chapter 13

Whilst examining himself in the mirror after showering, Joe did not notice any changes in his skin, or his general physique. Though he felt healthy, stronger than he had for years, and capable of getting through a day without having a nap. When he looked at his scalp, he was uncertain as to whether or not he saw a few faint strands of hair, in places where he was sure none should be. It was only because Lilly looked like she was getting physically younger, he hoped his fantasy would at least let him have his hair.

Since the return from the Hoola Joe spent most of his waking hours in the study. He found the study after his curiosity had turned him from the stairs in the landing, to the unexplored corridor. As soon as he had walked into the study, he had no interest in going any further. The room was large. He had entered the room from the landing door and it opened onto a balcony in front of a wall of bookshelves.

The room was a library more than a study, with shelves all the way around, filled with books. The shelves went so high on each level, there was a ladder on rails running along the tops of the shelves on both levels, allowing access to all the books.

He went to the ground floor of the study by stairs from the balcony. Opposite the ground floor door, in front of the wide windows that looked out to the back of the house, there was a desk of a grand scale. Despite its size, it was not out of proportion in the cavernous study. Long and wide, wooden tables went in pairs down the room with chairs around them. Plenty of space to spread out drawings and any other large documents.

There were plenty of writing and drafting materials. Joe could design almost anything with the books and equipment around him. Of all the things in the study, the only thing lacking was a computer.

There were numerous high blackboards around the room, covering the shelves and sliding across in front of them. Joe had to climb the ladder to write on them from the top. Other boards were scattered around the room, and he was covering them with calculations that he would never have attempted, except for his experience with the Hoola. There was an exchange of not only ideas, but ways of thinking that were influencing the theories that he had been working on at the university.

He had been made a professor a little later than most of his contemporaries. He blamed the delay in receiving his professorship in part on the loss of his wife, which had impacted him enormously. He also knew that there were other reasons why it had taken so long to achieve the recognition. He was cautious, and didn't take many of the chances that came his way. He didn't take the risks he should have, and that had held him back.

Joe pulled out the wallet that was in his pocket. He took out the picture he carried of his wife, a woman that was taken too soon from him and their sons. They had missed her intensely when she had gone, even though the last few months of her life were spent in a hospital bed, and she was unable to talk at the end. There were no goodbyes because when she was able to say goodbye, he would not allow it. He refused to believe she was dying, and was convinced that she would make a recovery. For a passionate woman she was very calm, and had not tried to make him understand. She had simply smiled and he saw the love in her eyes.

The mathematics on the boards was calling to him to continue his calculations, but instead he looked at the picture. He asked Sarah, "Why aren't you here?"

The silence was pure. After a moment he put the picture back in the wallet, and the wallet back in his trousers.

On his desk were flyers from detectives and he picked one which appealed to his eye more than the others. The title was 'Ed the Detective'. The biggest statement on the flyer after the title was 'Find lost Friends and Family'. It was then followed by 'Or did you die in mysterious circumstances?', 'Want to find an old foe?', 'Discover what happened behind your back' among other offers.

Joe scanned it to see where to go. Unfortunately, all it said was 'Hold the flyer to find me.' Just as Isaiah had done, when they went for pizza.

Clutching the flyer, Joe went down to see Isaiah, who was once again enjoying the sun on the patio. Lilly was with him. "Hello, Mr. Scientist, how go your studies?" asked Isaiah, he raised his hand, which was holding a reefer, and took a draw on it.

"How many of those did Lilly get?" asked Joe, pointing at the reefer.

"Only a few remain within her pouch."

"Could I have some of that?"

"Of course." Isaiah took another pull before passing the joint to Joe.

Taking a drag. "They're inconclusive," said Joe.

"What are inconclusive?"

"My studies."

"That's a shame," said Isaiah, taking a sip from his beer.

"There's something else I need to do," said Joe.

Isaiah was curious. "What do you need to do?"

Joe showed Isaiah the flyer. "I need to see this guy."

Isaiah studied the flyer. "What's a detective?" he asked.

"Someone who can find things and people."

"Aah," said Isaiah. "You think he could find your wife."

"Yes. What do you think?"

"There are many dead people, more than the living. You will need every help in your search."

"What if she doesn't want to be found?" asked Lilly.

"Why not? I know she would want me to find her," said Joe. Lilly took the joint from Joe.

"I had hoped to meet a friend when I died," said Isaiah. "But he was not here. My father and mother were not here, and none of my brothers or sisters. But I know others have met their kin." He chuckled. "It was all so long ago I no longer care."

"So, you think this is pointless?"

"I do not think it pointless, but before we go there is a matter of great import." Isaiah raised his beer and took a sip. He looked at the contents of the bottle. "But that will be concluded very soon."

Naturally before Isaiah finished his beer, something else came up. But Joe was determined and the delay was minimal.

Chapter 14

Joe kept a firm hold of the flyer as they walked, and as they walked Kal enquired about Joe's calculations and the ideas he had developed. Soon their conversation grew deep and involved.

After a while they were in a forest filled with tall trees, taller than the giant Redwoods of the Americas. Lichen grew on bark and blooms were appearing all around them. Butterflies and bees and birds could be heard flying through the air. The air was rich with delightful fragrances. They turned a path and were surprised to be stood before a palatial wooden cabin with a large sign at the edge of the path to the door, reading, "Ed the Detective." Then going on to list his services.

Walking to the main door, Joe knocked. The door was opened by a woman professionally dressed in a light grey suit. "Can I help you?" she asked happily.

"I'm here to see Ed," said Joe. "I need a detective."

"That's great," said the woman. Moving aside to let them in, she continued, "I'm Simi his assistant. Ed's just with a client and he'll be with you as soon as that's done."

They went into a living room with brown leather sofas, with tables and cabinets, and the decoration following a warm theme with earthy colours. The ceiling was high, and the lighting was low, given off by table lamps and wall lights. With its cosy atmosphere, Joe felt relaxed and at ease.

Simi asked them to take a seat. They sat in a set of sofas arranged around a large hearth. Simi's desk was past the sofas, with her seat backing up to the windows at the opposite end of the room to the fireplace.

In the opposite wall to the one they had come through, was a door which Joe assumed was Ed's office. Framed pictures of varying sizes were thoughtfully spaced around the door and over the rest of the wall. Over the fireplace was a painting dominating the room, of a city that looked like it belonged in the nineteen thirties. He did not recognize the location.

Simi offered drinks. Isaiah continued with the beers, and Lilly and Joe settled for a juice. Simi had offered them all a choice and explained she was learning to make cocktails, and Kal was eager to try a cocktail.

Simi was not particularly surprised to see an alien, though she had not seen one like Kal before and wanted to know all about his world. Once she had served the drinks the two of them went into a conversation of their own. Joe listened as she explained that former alien abductees had been to see Ed about finding the aliens who abducted them. Suppressed memories of their abductions had returned upon their deaths, and they were determined to find answers. Joe managed to bite his tongue throughout the whole exchange.

Meanwhile Isaiah took the opportunity to try his old-world charm on Lilly. It was strange to hear him talk of his great successes, whilst having the body and looks of a young man.

The door on the far side of the living room opened. A woman came out looking uncertain. The man stood behind her was in braces, without a jacket and wearing a tie, smoking a pipe and looking thoughtful.

"So she's in a commune?" said the woman.

"Yes," said Ed, in a gentle gravelly voice. "And I have to say she appears to be very happy."

"And she's a lesbian now?"

"She was always a lesbian. She just couldn't live as one when she was alive."

"Do you think she would want to see me?"

"All the information is in the file I gave you."

The woman looked at the file in her hands. It was thin, and when she opened it, there was a single sheet of paper.

"Oh my word, I did not expect any of this," said the woman studying the paper.

"She's your mother, I'm sure she'll be happy to see you. Don't take too long though, she's liable to move on at any time."

"You're right of course. Thank you for finding her for me. I don't know why I couldn't find her by myself."

"Don't worry about it. It's not as easy as it sounds and I've been doing this a long time."

"Oh my god. My poor father, what must he have thought when he got here?"

Ed smiled and said, "Maybe he never found out? Maybe he knew and they never told you. All questions you can ask your mother."

The woman stopped, seeing Joe and his friends, and was surprised by the sight of the floating Kal. "Oh my," she said. "What is that?"

"Yeah," said Ed. "I'm eager to find out."

Kal introduced himself and the woman responded with, "Oh that's wonderful. My first alien. I wish I could stay and chat with you, but I have to go." She turned to the detective, "I'll leave you to your clients, Ed, and I'll be back for my father."

Simi saw the client out and Ed turned to Joe and his friends. He put his hands under the straps of his braces. He looked over the group and being curious, asked, "Are you all together?"

They all nodded.

"I hope this is as interesting as it looks."

Ed invited them into his office, and the three of them just fitted into the sofa directly in front of his desk. There were seats to the sides but none of them thought of using them. Kal floated at the end of the sofa near Joe.

Ed was flanked by a variety of framed articles on his wall. There were various genres of books on shelves, and Joe noted there were many about genealogy and history. The history books were mostly modern, from around the first world war onwards.

"Now, tell me," said Ed, leaning back into his classic swivelling, wooden chair with brown leather covers, and lighting his pipe. The aroma from the pipe carried across to the four guests. They raised their noses curiously recognising the general scent.

"What could an alien, an ancient and a fresh young couple like you, want with me?"

Joe and Lilly looked at one another, when Ed said 'young couple'.

"We're not a couple," said Lilly. "Definitely not."

"My apologies," said Ed.

"It's just me," said Joe. "These guys came along for something to do, or out of curiosity."

Ed appeared intrigued. "Really?" he asked. "How do you know each other?"

Lilly explained immediately, "He killed me?" Pointing at Joe.

"It was an accident," objected Joe.

"Ruined one of the most important days of my life," continued Lilly.

Joe dropped his head shaking it in disbelief, and then held it in his hands.

"If I may interrupt," said Isaiah. "Ed, what is in your pipe?"

"Hashish," smiled Ed broadly.

"May I have some?" asked Isaiah.

"Sure," said Ed and opened a side drawer in his desk. He took out a slab of hashish and threw it over to Isaiah. Isaiah caught the block and sniffed it, whilst Kal extended a probe. Impressed, Isaiah raised his eyebrows and Kal broadcast his enthusiasm to try the hashish.

"You want some pipes?" asked Ed.

"I would indeed," said Isaiah.

Ed took out a wooden box from a cupboard and opening it presented it to Isaiah. Isaiah's eyes widened as he gazed upon the variety of beautifully crafted and polished pipes and chillums. "These are wondrous," said Isaiah, picking a pipe and handling it. "So beautifully crafted and shaped."

"So where were we?" said Ed taking his seat whilst Isaiah and Lilly picked some pipes. Then Ed realised Kal's biology made pipes awkward. He went to another cupboard and took out a large bong, with the bit connected by a flexible pipe to the main bowl. Kal expressed his appreciation.

"Now that we've established you both died at the same time," said Ed. "Why are you hanging around together?"

Joe raised his hands in wonder. "We both have to live in the same house?"

Ed looked to Lilly. "He killed you and now you're both living in the same house?"

Lilly shrugged. "Yeah, fucking crazy right?" she said.

"Apparently there wasn't any other accommodation available," said Joe.

Lilly had chosen a short pipe, and was waiting for Isaiah to pass on the hashish.

"What about you two?" Ed looked at Isaiah and Kal. "How do you know these two?"

Isaiah lit the hashish for Kal and then himself. With a lung full of smoke he explained, "I was in the Fields of Solitude when Joe wandered along and caught me in the middle of a disagreement with a parrot. Then I went back to his house with him and he let me stay."

Joe leaned forward and winking said quietly to Ed, "He only asked to stay because he thinks he has a chance with Lilly."

Joe leaned back, as Lilly spluttered and Isaiah continued, with plumes of smoke billowing out of his moth. "Then this fool said aliens didn't exist when I told him about the star people. He accused me of lying and so I took him to meet them. But we arrived at the planet of the Hoola."

Then Kal explained in his own way why he had come back with them and his mission to observe the ways of Humans.

"Fascinating," said Ed. "If we could just go back to something you said a moment ago. The Fields of Solitude?"

"A peaceful place for solitary contemplation. Very popular," said Isaiah.

Ed nodded, made a note and pursued the matter

no further. He turned to Joe and asked, "So what is it you want?"

"I'm looking for my wife," said Joe.

Ed sighed. "That's a shame," he said. "Seeing a group like yours made me hope for something new."

"Sorry to disappoint you," said Joe.

Ed waved away his disappointment. "Don't worry about it," he said. He picked up a fountain pen and opened his notebook. "So why are you looking for your wife?"

Joe was surprised by the question. "Because she's my wife and I want to see her."

"Are you sure she wants to see you?"

"Of course, she wants to see me!" Joe replied. "Why wouldn't she want to see me?"

"She's not here Joe, and you're looking for her. Maybe she doesn't want to be found."

"Now look here. I've been missing my wife for over twenty years, and when she died we were not angry with one another, we were more in love than the first day we met. Of course I want to see her, and I have no doubt she wants to see me."

"Twenty years?"

Joe nodded.

"That's a long time Joe."

"Yes, I know that."

"Maybe she moved on?"

Joe sighed. "Maybe," he said. "But I don't believe she has."

Ed leaned forward, lowered his pipe and said, "You

know when you die, for most people it's the end of everything and the start of something new?"

"So, what are you saying?" said Joe. "That it was all over when she died. That the bond we shared just vanished?"

"Mind you," said Lilly, having breathed out her smoke. "Don't forget you don't believe you're dead." Joe rolled his eyes.

Ed was surprised by Lilly's statement. "You think this is a dream?"

"Nothing that has happened fits with anything I was taught," Joe said firmly.

Ed laughed. "You're not kidding."

"Hell no," said Lilly.

"As I have said before, death was not what I expected either," said Isaiah. "But we knew little of death. We mostly feared there would be no god."

"And is there a god?" asked Joe. "You haven't met him."

"Or her," said Lilly.

Kal expressed his surprise at discovering the afterlife to all of them. With his telepathy it had all the impact and feelings of the actual moment.

"Didn't the sky people tell you?" scoffed Joe to Isaiah.

"You mock me?" said Isaiah. "You have also called me a liar. How dare you continue with such arrogance. Here is an alien," Isaiah emphasised the word alien. "Now you must apologise, if you have any substance about you."

Joe crossed his arms defiantly.

"Your word is worthless," said Isaiah, down his nose. "You are a low character."

"I am not!" said Joe.

"Hey calm down guys," said Ed, firmly. "You're in my house."

After several moments, "Well alright," said Joe. "You were right, there are aliens."

Isaiah drew on his pipe and looked at Joe patiently.

"Alright, I apologise for calling you a liar. I accept there are aliens. You were right, I was wrong."

Isaiah chuckled. "Did that hurt as much as it looked like it hurt?" he asked.

Joe crossed his arms again and looked forward in a huff. "Doesn't matter anyway," he mumbled. "You're just a figment of my imagination." This made Isaiah titter and tip towards little bursts of laughter whenever he looked at Joe.

Lilly leaned over towards Joe. "Oh, don't be such a baby," she said, with puppy dog eyes, and started to giggle. Kal sensing the humour joined in, in his own way, with his thought and fast trills. This only helped to make Isaiah laugh even more.

Joe turned away. With Kal's telepathy it was hard to ignore the humour.

"If this is a fantasy Joe, you could just imagine your wife into your dream," said Ed, somehow just managing to avoid being sucked in by the infectious laughter.

"As I have already stated," Joe turned and glanced

at Lilly. "I don't control my dreams. And this isn't just an ordinary dream, I had a major car accident. I must be in some kind of coma."

Ed considered for a moment. "So you're just playing along?"

"If you like," said Joe. He ignored Isaiah's chuckle.

"Hey wait a fucking minute," said Lilly. "I just thought of something. What if I'm not dead either and I'm in a coma too, and we're like sharing the same fucking fantasy?"

"Oh for the sake of all things holy, that's just ridiculous!" said Joe.

They all continued to laugh even more, and could not hold themselves back. When they finally calmed down, Joe sighed and asked, "Could we just get on with why I'm here now?"

"Ok," smiled Ed. He relit his pipe, took a drag and let it out "I guess I can play along too." The others smirked.

Straightening himself up Ed continued. "In twenty years, you kept true to your wife?" he asked. The scepticism in his voice made Joe instantly uncomfortable.

Joe looked at Lilly, Isaiah and Kal, and all three once again looked back at him eager to hear what he would say. "Well..." started Joe. He stuttered, and realising his pause had given away the truth said, "I had occasional needs. I'm no angel."

"And what if she had similar needs?"

After a long pause, whilst his companions waited patiently to hear his reply, with stoned easy and happy smiles, Joe said, "I can't hold that against her. I had my opportunities but I could never get her out of my mind, and I know she felt the same way about me."

"Really? Twenty years changes people Joe," said Ed.

"I know that!"

"And you know she won't be the same person anymore?"

"Of course. But at the core, I know who she is, I know how she truly felt about me. Deep inside."

"And you know the afterlife is a big place? I mean an infinitely big place."

Frustrated Joe decided to put an end to this line of questioning. "Look are you going to help me find my wife or not?"

"Alright, alright," said Ed. "I just want to be sure you understand the situation. It's not easy finding someone when they recently died, never mind going as far back as this. But as it's your fantasy maybe I'll get lucky."

Joe snorted. The others tittered.

Ed emptied his pipe of ash into an ashtray. "So, tell me about your wife," he said.

Joe described his wife and showed the picture he kept in his wallet. His friends curiously looked over his shoulder, to see what this amazing woman looked like. Isaiah raised eyebrows nodding approvingly, Lilly shrugged her shoulders dismissively and Kal was unmoved. Ed got up to get a copy of the picture.

Joe turned to his friends and said, "This could take a while. Why don't I catch up with you later?"

Lilly immediately stood up. "Great idea," she said. "This has become incredibly dull."

"Indeed," said Isaiah standing up and putting on his sunglasses. He turned to Kal. "Would you like to join me? I intend to find somewhere to drink."

Kal was tempted but was more interested in what Joe was doing.

Lilly and Isaiah put their used pipes on the desk before leaving. Isaiah asked Ed for some of the hashish and Ed happily broke off a chunk.

After Isaiah and Lilly left, Joe continued to talk about his wife to Ed, explaining her family and background. The books on genealogy made more sense as Joe went into detail.

"That's useful," said Ed. "What were her political beliefs?"

"Political beliefs?"

"Yeah, it'll give me some ideas of where to start. Maybe she went looking for world leaders she admired?"

"Of course," said Joe. "She was a passionate woman. There are leaders she admired, writers too, and answers she would look for."

Joe didn't tell Ed everything he recalled, only what he thought was pertinent. He explained what he thought were his wife's personal beliefs. He spoke of her interests and hobbies and the places she wanted to visit, her family and whatever else he could think of. He remembered the first time they met.

Like a fly on the wall, Joe saw the events of his past

played out before him. Stupid and serious arguments, and times when he and Sarah were in complete agreement. Fortunately, the latter outweighed the former by many times.

When they finished, Joe and Ed stood up. Ed refilled his pipe, offering a lump to Kal, sensing his desire, and walked Joe with Kal to the door. "Listen," said Ed, "even if you could tell me every last thing about your wife, this won't be easy. You're new and you've discovered another world already." He looked towards Kal. "Imagine what she could do in 20 years. Anything's possible."

"As true as that may be," said Joe. "I have to try. How long before I come back to you? And what do I owe you?"

"Don't worry about that," said Ed. "You may have noticed there's no money here, so maybe I'll need something from you one day."

"Are you sure," said Joe.

Ed smiled and spread his arms. "Hey, I love what I do," he said. "Why else would I do it?"

"So, when you say you may need something from me one day, what exactly does that mean?"

Ed laughed. "It doesn't mean anything," he said. "I don't wear a black suit, and I'm not a mobster. There aren't any strings attached. I'm good at what I do and I'll keep doing it until I get bored."

"That's really generous of you," said Joe.

"Go home, have a drink, enjoy a smoke, or whatever

you're into. I'll get started, and when you come back, I should have something for you."

Joe and Kal took their leave and as they walked Kal asked, "You spoke of a bond. Is this something that you can feel? Perhaps like my telepathy?"

"It's not something you feel or sense like telepathy," said Joe after a moment of thought. "It's a feeling you have. It's a connection. like an understanding, or an appreciation."

For a few moments Joe walked in silence and Kal said quietly, "I sensed your appreciation of your wife."

When they were back at the house only Isaiah was home. He was in the living room with an open bottle of whisky. Joe noted it was a single malt. He wondered for a second why he had such wonderful produce in the house. Isaiah stood up to say hello, but staggered and fell flat on the ground. Joe and Kal helped to pick him up. With their help Isaiah got to his feet without having to let go of the bottle.

"This is no wine," slurred Isaiah. "I had something similar before. It too was delightful."

Isaiah returned to his seat, and Joe joined him on the sofa.

"Did you find your wife?" asked Isaiah. His eyes were barely able to focus on Joe. He appeared to be looking into the distance.

"No," said Joe. "Ed hasn't started the search yet."

Joe got up and got two tumblers from the drinks cabinet and said, "Can we have some of that?" But

Isaiah's head had fallen back and his eyes were closed. Joe reached over and prised the bottle of whisky out of Isaiah's hand.

Pouring the whisky into the two tumblers, Joe pushed one over to Kal. Kal reached out with a tentacle and inspected the crystal glass. Joe held up the tumbler, and Kal did the same. Joe reached over to touch the glasses, and said, "Here's to finding Sarah."

They both took a sip and relaxed. The warmth of the whisky gently flowed down Joe's throat and outwards from his stomach. With the lights low, in silence, they looked out of the high wall of glass into the valley, with the patchy clouds under a blanket of stars. Among the trees there was the occasional flash, and the sound of thunder. Joe ignored some of the unusual shapes he saw in the sky, and instead allowed himself to be wrapped in the warmth of the whisky, as did Kal.

"I wonder where Lilly is," said Joe. Kal gave him a mental shrug and they enjoyed the rest of the whisky in silence.

After a while Joe looked around and seeing the house was in a mess they began to clean up. Isaiah managed to sleep through it all.

Chapter 15

A bottle of wine was clenched in Isaiah's hand as he slept on the sofa. Kal and Joe had savoured the whisky. It was definitely a drink that was best appreciated at a gentle pace.

Recalling the day before, Joe remembered the series of memories which had surfaced during the meeting with Ed. Like Lilly, some of those memories had been quashed and stuck in a dark corner of his mind, and he experienced personal discomfort at their recollection.

Kal was floating in the darker, high corner of the living room, his colours diminished and barely visible. Going to the kitchen Joe turned on the coffee machine and he heard Isaiah shout from the living room. "Joe, I too shall have coffee."

Joe sensed Kal wake up as well, more from Isaiah's shouting than from the sound of the coffee machine.

Joe made coffee for all of them and Isaiah and Kal joined him at the breakfast table. "Where's Lilly?" he asked.

"After much drinking, during which she brooded

greatly, we returned and she spoke of a need to be alone," said Isaiah. "She went for a walk."

"Wonder where she went," said Joe. "I hope she's alright."

"Why? What do you fear?" asked Isaiah.

"I don't know," said Joe. "I would hate to imagine anything bad happening to her. And she's a woman out on her own. She might run into some unsavoury characters?"

"Unsavoury characters?" said Isaiah. "What an odd expression. But don't worry. It's impossible for her to come to any direct harm from another."

"I find your lack of concern troubling," said Joe sternly. "She's not a big lady. Do you think she's capable of fighting off a determined assailant?"

Isaiah leaned in to look directly at Joe, appearing mildly amused. "Weren't you told about the rules of the afterlife?"

"Dan mentioned that you couldn't hurt anyone directly, physically."

"Do not doubt his word on the matter. You worry unnecessarily, no harm will come to her body. I fear for any being who would attack her with only their words as weapons."

Joe and Kal laughed. "Ok," said Joe. "But what if someone does try to attack her, and there's no one around to protect her?"

Isaiah's smile broadened. "If such a situation should arise," he asked, "would you protect her?"

"Well of course. I may not be much, but I would do the best I could. Wouldn't you?"

"Yes, if I could I would. But I would not have to."

"Why not?"

"Because the dark one will take care of it."

Joe was exasperated. "But what if the dark one is not around?"

Isaiah laughed. "When the need arises, he will arrive Joe. They can sense a moment about to occur. Somehow, they are wherever they need to be, moving faster than the eye can see. And if they should catch the criminal... well you should understand one does not want to be caught by those beings in black robes."

Kal took a sip of the coffee and his tentacles flayed, exploding a variety of colours, breaking their usual symmetry.

At that point there was a knock at the door. Whilst Kal calmed himself from his first sip of the coffee, Joe went to the main door and shoved aside the pile of new flyers again. On the other side of the door was a young man, very smartly dressed, in a tweed jacket, and cream flannel trousers. Joe could not help thinking how incredibly good looking he was.

"Hello," said the young man.

"How can I help you, young man?" asked Joe.

"'Young man'," the visitor laughed." Fuckin' 'ell, nice o' you t' say so. 'aven't 'eard that in a while. I was wonderin' if Miss Lilly was 'ome?"

"Miss Lilly?"

"Yeah. Met 'er last night. Delightful she was, I 'ad to call on 'er."

"Are you sure you have the right house?"

"Oh yeah. I made sure I got all the details. You'd be Joe. The fella who killed 'er."

Joe was caught off guard. "I'm Joe. Who might you be?"

"I'm Sing."

"Sing?"

"Sing."

"Ok, if you say so. Look Lilly's not here."

"Please tell 'er I called and I'll be back," he pondered for a few seconds, "maybe tomorro'?"

"Whatever you like," said Joe.

"And before I go a word of advice," said Sing, smiling. "Make the most of that bald patch, the white hair and the wrinkles. It soon goes, so get out there and don't waste a fuckin' moment young man." He emphasised the 'young man'.

Whilst Joe was lost for words Sing said, "See ya," and was gone. Joe shut the door and quietly walked back to the kitchen.

"You look confused," said Isaiah.

"What is it that makes no sense?" asked Kal.

Joe replayed the scene to Kal, and Kal expressed his amusement. Isaiah was more concerned about Sing. "So, he was here seeking Lilly?"

"Yes," laughed Joe. "I mean what's that all about? He was eager. He'll be back."

A low "Hmm," came from Isaiah. He appeared grim and stony, as his eyes were hooded by his brows. "When he returns, I will be sure to make him understand he should return to whatever swamp he might dwell in," said Isaiah.

Joe laughed and Kal was amused. "Why do you laugh?" asked Isaiah.

"You said it yourself," said Joe. "What can you do? You can't do anything physically. Anyway, I don't think Lilly would be interested in him. You have a better chance."

Isaiah's mood changed instantly. "Truly?" he asked.

"Not much better, but better."

Kal flickered with mirth.

Joe got up and asked Kal, "Would you join me for some further theorising? I've had some new ideas."

Kal was happy to join Joe whilst Isaiah went to watch the magic on the big screen.

Lost in the world of mathematics, Joe barely noticed Kal turn away from the formulas. It was when Kal was at the door that Joe turned and asked, "You had enough?"

Kal had not had enough, but was distracted by a disturbance downstairs. Curious, Joe followed Kal. They went to the living room and, as they rounded the corner, saw Isaiah on the sofa facing the large blank, which made a giant screen for the projector they had discovered, crying.

"What's wrong?" asked Joe.

"This story," said Isaiah, still bubbling. "It's so sad."

Before they could go any further, Kal brightened and said, "Lilly is returning."

Isaiah jumped up. Joe heard the front door open, followed by Lilly's grunt as she pushed aside the flyers with the door to get in. Isaiah flew by Joe and Kal towards the kitchen, through the dining room, as Lilly came through the door to the living room. She immediately turned to Joe and excitedly said, "Guess who I met."

"Who?"

"Remember the old guy and the young guy when we went through processing?"

"You met them?"

"Yeah. They got a house together as well. They're having a great time."

Joe and Lilly went to the dining table to sit down. Isaiah returned from the kitchen wiping his face.

"How did you meet them?" asked Joe.

"When I was out walking yesterday. I saw something moving in the bushes, and it was the old guy with... a friend. They were going like rabbits. They didn't even notice I was there."

"Really?" said Joe, a little shocked.

"Oh yeah," said Lilly. Kal was intrigued. "I cleared my throat and all they did was look round and smile at me. Just kept going."

"Wow. Just like that couple in the garden."

"You've got a real outdoorsy theme going there, Joe," said Lilly, laughing.

"What happened in the garden?" asked Isaiah.

"There was a couple making love at the edge of the forest," said Joe.

"Hmm," said Isaiah. "Making love in nature is wonderful."

Lilly and Joe could only look at one another as Isaiah's gaze wandered into the distance, Kal flickered with Isaiah's thoughts.

"What did you do?" Joe asked Lilly.

"I left them to it. I walked along the path a little further on and I saw Kai sitting on a rock looking across some fields. Their names are Si and Kai, by the way. He was waiting for Si to finish. Turns out the woman saw Si heading home with Kai, and just came on to him. Couldn't resist the wrinkles. Kai says he gets propositioned all the time, and just doesn't know how to say no."

Isaiah said, "Intelligent man." He sat down next to Joe.

"Doesn't sound like you have to be smart. Kai looked pissed off when he told me about Si's luck. Anyway, they invited us over."

"What like for dinner or something?"

"I don't know. They just said come over sometime."

"That's nice," said Joe. "So, what else did you do for the rest of the night?" asked Joe.

"Oh, I went to their house. Si finished and they invited me back. We should go, that boy can put some combos together."

"Combos?" asked Isaiah.

"Combinations," explained Lilly. "You know, a little bit of this, a little bit of that. That boy's got a touch."

"Is that where you met Sing?" asked Joe.

"Yes," said Lilly. "Was he here?"

"Yes," said Isaiah ominously.

"Was there a problem?" asked Lilly.

"No problem," said Joe. "I think he was quite taken with you."

"Yeah, he was hanging around me for a while. I didn't really go for that accent. But fuck he sure knew what to say."

Lilly continued. "What about you?" she asked Joe. "How did it finish with the detective?"

"He's going to start the search, but he's not very hopeful. It's been such a long time Sarah could be anywhere."

"Oh dear," said Lilly. "So, he might not find her?"

"Tell me," said Isaiah. "I wish to understand. If this is your fantasy, you must surely find her? If you should succeed, how will it prove that this is real? Surely it must only prove you right about everything being a creation of your imagination?"

Joe looked around at each of them and said, "It just will. I will know, and that's all that matters."

There was the click of a lighter and Joe, Lilly and Isaiah turned to Kal as he lit the hashish in the tall bong. Joe had not noticed him prepare the bong and he couldn't work out how he would do it without fingers, especially crumbling the lumps into the bowl.

But he was happy when Kal passed the bit around, and stopped wondering where Kal had found the bong.

After a few minutes Isaiah turned to Joe and said, "I wish to help you, Joe. I will help you find your wife."

"You will?" said Joe.

"Yes. It would please me to help you, and I would like to meet this amazing woman who can hold your heart for so long."

"Oh yeah," said Lilly. "She must be an amazing woman."

Isaiah stood up. "We can all help," he said. "Let us start our search today."

The others all nodded their agreement. "Yeah," said Lilly.

"Good," stated Isaiah. "We shall start today. And I know where we should start."

"You do?" asked Joe.

"Of course. She was a Jew, was she not?"

"Yes."

"Then we will go and search among our fellow Jews."

Joe laughed. "Oh my god that's actually a good idea. And it's something to do." He took a draw. Isaiah sat down next to him and took the pipe. "You want to get going?" asked Joe. Isaiah hummed his agreement as he took a lung full of the pungent smoke. Then Kal passed Lilly the bit, she took a drag and stared into space.

After a few minutes Lilly asked, "Anyone want some chips?" Everyone eagerly accepted her offer.

It took an undefinable amount of time longer before they managed to leave the house. They needed to prepare a bowl for that. Eventually they were walking once again, and this time down the valley. Once they reached the edge of the forest they were in open land. There were other houses they saw on the way, and occasionally they waved to people they saw. Kal shot off to meet the other humans with mixed reactions. Isaiah did not stop for any of them, he kept moving.

The temperature rose, shrubs and bushes became more common, and the trees were spread out in smaller groups.

"You know what?" said Joe.

"What?" said Lilly.

"Have you seen the people flying?"

"I noticed."

"I was wondering if we could do that."

Lilly paused for a moment. "That's true," she said. "If they can, why can't we? Hey, you've had flying dreams before, right?"

"Yes."

"So why don't you dream yourself flying? And us while you're at it. I think I'd enjoy that."

Joe gave Lilly an irritated look.

"What?" asked Lilly innocently.

"It's not that kind of dream."

"What kind of dream is it, Joe?"

Joe walked a little faster ahead of Lilly, he did not want to turn around to see the smug expression on her face. Then she asked him, "Hey, why don't we ask Isaiah?"

"What do you mean?"

"He's been here for a long time. I bet he knows how to fly."

"Why didn't I think of that?"

"Maybe you just did."

Joe sped up and approached Isaiah. "Hey Isaiah, can you fly?"

"Yes," said Isaiah, without breaking his pace.

"You can? Can you teach us?"

"No."

"Why not?"

"It is not easily explained. Some seem to learn quickly, others use meditation and may take many years to merely levitate. Some will even throw themselves from cliffs and allow their instincts to provide the solution. There are many ways to learn."

"So, I have to work it out for myself?"

"Perhaps. You may meet one who can teach you."

"Like whom?"

"Perhaps some monks might help. Like those of the Eastern Mountains, who live about The Hundred peaks."

Cresting a hill Joe did not pursue the subject of flying any further, as before them was spread a colony. At first Joe was disappointed, since the colony was small, but then he realised that this was one colony and he could see many more in the distance. And the sky was full of a variety of flying or floating things.

"Here we are," said Isaiah. "Let us find refreshments?"

They quickly found a coffee stop. "Aah," breathed Isaiah, as he reclined on his seat and sipped from his cup.

Kal had a cup on the table on one side for him, and his three companions were sat in the other three places enjoying their coffees. Kal lifted the cup to his mouth and took a sip. He immediately withdrew and exploded into an array of colours that gave his companions the image of someone scrunching their face and tightening their shoulders. Kal's reaction was just as strong as the first time he had tried coffee.

Joe did not understand why Kal drank the coffee, when he had such a strong reaction to it. Because Kal did not share the sensations he felt, Joe assumed he must not have liked it. He wondered if Kal just wanted to keep the feeling to himself, and in truth he thoroughly relished the coffee.

"I'd say it's a coffee shop," said Joe, "but we didn't pay for anything."

"Nope," said Lilly. "Wish it was like that when I was alive."

"So why do it? Why operate a coffee... place, if you don't get anything out of it? Like the Pizza. And Ed."

"You think coin is the only reason to do anything?" said Isaiah. "Maybe it is the making and sharing that gives satisfaction? Even this moderate coffee pleases me, and so it should please the one who made it."

Lilly and Joe looked at Isaiah, shocked by his last

statement. Kal floated down facing Isaiah. "There's better coffee than this?" asked Lilly.

"It's true," said Isaiah. "I have met some who made coffee far better than this."

"Can't imagine it getting better than this," said Joe.

"Oh no way," agreed Lilly.

"Now you're just messing with me," said Joe.

"Messing with you? What do you mean by that?"

"Oh, come on," said Joe. "'Moderate' coffee? Really?"

Isaiah was offended. "What makes you think you know better? How long have you been dead?"

Joe stood up, "What does it matter how long I might or might not have been dead? I can tell a good coffee from an excellent coffee just as well as you, and this is excellent coffee!"

Isaiah stood up and said, "And you are so filled with wonder at all that you eat and taste, you cannot yet sense the mediocre from the good and the excellent." They faced off against each other.

Lilly calmly watched the exchange. "Are you two going to fight?" she asked. "Because I don't think you should. Especially you Joe, Isaiah would beat you."

Joe was stood firm, a grey haired balding septuagenarian facing off against an ancient warrior, trained to kill and accomplished in all forms of combat and warfare. Joe did not care about his disadvantage. Lilly's goading made him clench a fist, and as he prepared to throw a punch a familiar aroma drifted over to Joe. He sniffed the air a little harder and turned to see Dude and Dan walking towards them.

"Hey guys, what are you doing here?" asked Lilly.

Joe instinctively stepped away from Isaiah. They sat back down and turned to Dude and Dan.

Dude asked sternly, "Joe man, y' clenching your fist t' say hello?"

"Why do you care?" asked Joe. "I should punch this guy in the face."

"Now I wouldn't go doing that," said Dan, almost sounding like he hoped Joe would. "That's some bad mojo."

"Oh really?" scoffed Joe. Isaiah remained silent.

When Dan laughed it was a deep and resonant sound, and carried an ominous note that made Joe pause.

Dude drew on his joint and exhaled slowly. He looked at Dan who smiled knowingly, his frightful mask slipped away.

"Pay attention man," said Dude, with warm tones of understanding. "If the man Dan says don't be doin' that, y' best not be doin' it."

"Or what?" asked Joe.

"Punishment," said Dude.

Joe looked at Dan, and in a moment the light around him faded and the black suit did not seem dark enough.

Joe looked away and saw the others do the same.

"Don't worry about it," said Isaiah to Joe, lifting his cup. "If this is the best your imagination can do, it will suffice."

"Oh, very funny," said Joe.

Dude considered the two men. "What are y' fightin' about?"

Laughing, Lilly answered the question. "Coffee?" she said and explained.

"You're arguing over the quality of the coffee?" asked an incredulous Dude.

"Dan man, grab that chair for me," said Dude.

Dan pulled up a chair and sat down. Dude tutted and muttered and grabbed another chair.

"The coffee smells good," said Dude. "I think maybe I should see for myself." He turned to Dan, "Dan how about y' get us some coffee?"

"Get your own coffee," said Dan.

"Oh come man, stop your sulking. Y' been in this game too long for all that nonsense."

"I'm busy," said Dan, and pulled out a box from an inside pocket of his jacket and a bag of bud from another.

Isaiah stood up and said, "I shall fetch your coffee if it will stop your bickering."

"Black no sugar," said Dude.

"Latte with lots of sugar," said Dan, breaking off little pieces of bud into the paper for his joint. Kal had floated down to examine Dan's bud.

"So, what are you doing here anyway?" asked Joe.

"I feel the pull 'n' I go where it takes me," said Dude.

"And that mysterious force brought you here?"

"Yes man. 'n' now I feel like enjoyin' a nice cup o' coffee with you 'n' Lilly 'n' Isaiah and," he looked closely at the alien, "the Hoola."

Lilly smiled at Dude. "I'm glad you feel that way," she said.

Isaiah returned with the two coffees for Dude and Dan. He sniffed the air. "That is an interesting aroma," he said.

Dan passed the Joint to Isaiah and leaned back. "Indeed it is," he grinned. "What're y'all doing here anyway?"

"Isaiah offered to help me search for my wife," said Joe.

"You a detective now Isaiah?" asked Dan.

Isaiah squeezed Dan's shoulder. "My dear deadly friend, you know how chance can be generous when a man grasps the challenge."

"Take the hand away," ordered Dan simply.

Isaiah immediately removed his hand and spread his arms saying, "Relax. I'm merely being friendly."

Dude asked, "So y' thought y'd come t' your people t' start."

Joe nodded.

"Jah. Y' got the tough job man." Dude sucked in air.

"Do you know how many Jews have died through-out history?" asked Dan.

"Look, my wife was always more interested in her faith more than me," said Joe. "She would want to meet her people and I know she would've gone look-ing for her mother and father."

"Well alright. Good luck with that," said Dan, easing back into his seat.

"Actually," said Joe. "Now that we're here, what should we do next?" He looked at Isaiah.

"Now we must use what you know of your wife to find her," said Isaiah.

"Well. I suppose we should start by finding people who might've died about the same time. Or maybe look for some family lines." Joe looked around and up into the sky. "Where's Kal?" he asked. "He's pretty good on this sort of thing."

"He was here just a minute ago," said Lilly, suddenly very concerned. "I hope he's ok."

"Over there," said Isaiah, pointing above the trees and houses. They spotted the growing dot that was Kal, approaching in the distance. He was soon with them.

"I sensed concern," communicated Kal.

"Where did you go?" asked Lilly. "We got worried when we couldn't see you."

"Fear not," said Kal. "I was merely watching humans in an act of procreation."

An image flashed into their minds. A look of shock came over Lilly's face, Joe's jaw dropped, and Isaiah grinned and said, "That's not an act of procreation, that's an orgy."

"Orgy?" asked Kal.

"Let me explain," said Isaiah, looking into Kal.

"Aah," said Kal, as he shimmered and his fins shook, with understanding and delight emanating from him. "Interesting."

"Can you tell me where this orgy might be taking place?" asked Isaiah.

"It is finished," said Kal. Images of the end of the orgy flashed into everyone's minds. Lilly and Joe gasped and Isaiah laughed. "Is it possible to fertilize the females orally?" asked Kal. "Without more detail of the anatomy ..."

"No!" said Lilly.

Chapter 16

Kal was eager to work out a strategy for the search and as he discussed the plan with Joe and Isaiah, Lilly got bored and looked at Dan's box. There was a pipe and hashish inside, and Dan happily filled it for her.

"That is some good shit," said Lilly easing back into her seat. "Ed's was good shit too, but the two are so fucking distinct. It's like they've got their own personalities. Man!"

Dan and Dude paid close attention to what Joe, Kal and Isaiah were discussing. Whilst they worked Joe noticed Kal becoming steadily more and more distracted.

Isaiah held out a loaded pipe to Joe. "I don't know if that's a good idea," said Joe. Before Isaiah could answer, a quick tentacle took the pipe from his hand, and Kal asked, "Please light this." By angling the pipe in a certain way, Kal had found a method of smoking from without getting burnt.

Laughing, Isaiah lit the hash and Kal pulled hard on the pipe. As the contents were burnt out the smoke was blown out of the gills behind Kal's front fins, and with a mental sigh Kal's colours returned to a gentle steady rhythm. He shared the feeling with his companions. They all slouched deeper into their seats with happy grins.

After a while Dan stood up and went to get some drinks from the café. He returned with fruit juices. Joe took a sip and then drank it all down quickly. Kal had slowly floated up, swaying back and forth. Lilly shouted up to him and he calmly floated down, and like Joe took a sip and then finished the drink in one more draw.

Then Kal rose up again, and this time he was looking into the distance in a specific direction.

"What is it?" asked Joe.

"It is a great concentration of thought. So many minds are focused upon one place and one person," said Kal. "I sensed it in the distance, and it has grown stronger whilst we planned."

"Really?" asked Joe.

"So many minds," said Kal.

"What do you think it is?" asked Lilly.

"I must go there," said Kal.

The rest of the group looked around at one another. "I guess we better go there," smiled Joe.

They finished their drinks and followed Kal as he floated away ahead of them, pulled along by his curiosity.

As they walked, they noticed great square towers in the distance, rising straight up into the sky. Getting closer to the towers the crowds began to grow larger.

The average age group of the crowds was growing too. There were tents appearing in clusters, and people offering food to take away. The place started to appear like a festival site. Then Joe noticed that there was a theme. There were bands and choirs, some set up casually as they walked, others on makeshift stages, and then there were the professional looking stages with large crowds, all singing Christian songs. Watching Christians head banging to a heavy metal version of 'How Great Thou Art' was a truly mind bending experience.

At times they passed masses on their knees being led by priests in prayer. Some had set up large tables with religious paraphernalia. Sometimes there were groups stood chanting. Hymns could be heard in various accents in all directions, but strongest of all within the densest parts of the crowd.

The songs and praise were punctuated with the sound of screaming and shouting. There was that familiar crack of lightning, and smoke and flashes were visible from various parts of the crowds, as the occasional person was seen blasted into the air.

There were many dark suited beings with their partners. Dude and Dan gave a wave of the hand to their fellows as they caught one another's eye.

Dan looked excited in the charged atmosphere. There was an enormous tension in the air mixed with the dedication of the religious. There were various sects and they were happily expressing their biases and opinions. There were Catholics and Protestants and a whole variety of other denominations. As they passed, the groups would shout and heckle one another. Insults were regularly thrown back and forth, and just as they goaded one another into action they would pull back at the last minute, glancing at those in the dark suits who were grinning with eager anticipation.

Then Joe noticed some Arabs in the crowd. They appeared to be in a heated discussion with a variety of people.

Joe heard one of them shout, "This is a Christian crowd, not a place for terrorists."

"You're a bigot," came the reply. "You're terrorists too. You just call it something else."

The masses moved Joe and his friends on, before he could hear anymore. The hustle and bustle and the noise intensified.

There was a platform set up with a group of people preaching to the crowd and telling them to give up their pilgrimage. Banners read, "Jesus does not know you." "He does not need your worship." "Jesus is not the son of God." There were other banners, and the crowd would tear down one, and another would quickly replace it.

The crowd before the platform was seething with rage. It could be felt as Joe approached the stage. There was an intensity of screams and shouts as the dark ones revelled in their work.

At another platform the speaker told them their faith was misguided. The pilgrims should embrace the new reality, and join the New Church of the Resurrected.

Shouts of, "Heretics," could be heard. A petrol bomb was suddenly seen flying through the air, and was intercepted by a demon. The bottle exploded and the flames were gathered into a ball of fire, and returned to the sender, who screamed in agony. Dark ones laughed and clapped.

Joe and his friends quickly moved away from the hostile crowds, whilst Dan sought to linger for an opportunity to exercise his given talents. Dude pulled him away.

As they went deeper into the crowd, occasional gift stalls appeared with a variety of Christian memorabilia. Every one eagerly doing their best to give away their wares.

The towers Joe had noticed, could be seen to be rising hundreds of metres into the air.

"I thought this was a Jewish area," said Joe.

"It is man," said Dude.

"But it seems like some kind of Christian festival?"

"Hey Joe," said Dan. "How about you shout out you're a Jew? Tell all o' these folk to fuck off."

Then Dude spoke with a drop in his voice, filled with authority. "Chah, Dan man. Y' want t' stop takin' liberties. Y' already got that big mark against y' with Joe's cousin Deb. And I'm turnin' a blind eye with a lot o' your nonsense."

Dan glared at Dude. The sudden tension between them was palpable. They were still for several seconds before they backed away and the situation was over as quickly as it had begun.

"So what are all these Christians doing here?" asked Joe. "Is there the mother of all churches down there or something?"

"No," said Dan. "The mother of all churches is over there."

They all turned and looked in the direction Dan was pointing. They looked in awe at the structure that was being built in the distance. There were thousands of people, tiny in the foreground to one corner of the structure, which was made up of stones that must have weighed hundreds of tons each. From the scale, Joe estimated the base was not even a quarter built.

"What are those?" asked Lilly, pointing at the tall square towers.

"Observation towers," said Dan.

"What the fuck are they looking at?"

"Jesus house," said Dude.

"Jesus? You mean Jesus Christ, Jesus?"

"Who else?"

Joe looked at Dude. "No," he gasped wide eyed.

Dude and Dan looked at one another. "Been a long time," pointed out Dude.

"Yep," said Dan. "These two are taking us places we haven't been for many lifetimes."

"I thought this was a Jewish area?" said Joe.

"Y' already said that. You know Jesus was a Jew, right?"

"Yes, but..." Joe looked at the crowds.

"Don't forget those Muslims you saw earlier," said Lilly.

"Yep. To them he's a prophet. Up there with Mohammed," said Dan.

"You know what?" said Dan to Dude.

"Yes man," smiled Dude.

Joe tried to look over the crowd. "Hey Kal," he shouted up. "How far does this crowd go?"

Kal turned and looked around. "These masses go as far as I can see," he said. "I cannot say how far they go."

"There's millions of them," said Joe.

"Would you like to meet him?" asked Dan.

"What? Jesus? Oh hell yes," said Lilly.

"I'd like to see him again," said Isaiah. Then he observed, "These crowds are many times larger than I remember. It will take another age to get through them to his hidden entrance."

"No," said Dan. "Not that long."

"Come," said Dude. Dude and Dan turned and walked away from the crowds. Joe started to laugh as they turned to leave. To his mind he had just heard as much confirmation of the fantasy as he could.

There was a shout from the side and Joe turned to see an elderly woman stood in shock, with her hands to her mouth. There was rustling from a bush and an equally elderly man stood up naked. "Ah yes dear," said the man, nervously. "Was there something you needed?"

A handsome young man stood up behind him, also naked.

"What are you doing?" asked the woman.

"This young man was just showing me some interesting flowers dear."

"And you had to get undressed to do that?"

The old man sighed. "Umm. Well. You know how I've always been a bit more broadminded..."

"Broadminded? BROADMINDED?"

"Darling, you know it's not like we have any obligations now. It was 'till death do us part' after all."

The woman was dumbstruck.

The young man spoke up. "Damn you're hot," he said.

"What?" said the woman.

"Why don't you join us?" He walked up to the old woman and placed the palm of his hand on her shoulder. She was taken aback and pushed the young man's hand away.

The old woman looked back at the old man. "But all those years we were married. We have children," she said.

"And I love them. And you. But you know I've always had needs."

"NEEDS? You've done this before? When we were alive?"

"Yes, but now we're dead dear," said the old man. "Maybe we should move on from our lives?"

The old woman was enraged and pointing towards the mass of people, she said. "Our Lord Jesus is over there. What would he think of what you're doing? You are a sinner, dear." She said the 'dear' with as much vitriol as she could muster. "You must be judged for your sin, by God's law."

"Sodomites!" shouted the old woman.

"Now calm down dear," said the old man.

Other members of the crowd looked over at the commotion. One of them pointed and shouted, "Sinners! Children of Sodom!"

Dan turned to see what would happen. They all watched as parts of the crowd started to march towards the couple. The old man was frozen to the spot, and the young man watched unperturbed by the danger heading towards him. The older man started to back away in fear.

A group of Dan's dark suited brothers and sisters were eagerly preparing along the edges. The shout ran through the crowd, and a mob began to form. Dan smiled and started to move towards the unfolding trouble, when Dude grabbed him by the shoulder and pulled him away. "Not now man," said Dude. "We're goin' t' see Jesus."

Dan turned to Dude, furious. "Are you out of your mind?" said Dan. "There's a mob about to go nuts and I'm right next to it, and you want me to leave?"

"Yeah man. Leave it t' their folk. Y' got plenty action already."

"Fuck we have," said Dan, angrily.

"Y' got a complaint y' know what to do."

"All I been getting lately is a few simple disagreements. We've had nothing but accidents and natural disasters lately."

"Consider it penance for your indiscretions."

Dan turned to leave but continued to complain. "In the middle of a religious hotspot and I got to ignore all the action. Got the whole universe and more, and I don't get to see a war zone in how long?"

The others followed, with a large bang behind them, and the sound of the pilgrims screaming. Joe could see the disappointment on Dan's face as they walked and listened to the noises. A shout came out from the commotion to be clearly heard, "Hey Dan, this one's for you," followed by intense screaming. Without turning Dan shouted, "Fuck you, Joy!"

Slowly the crowds thinned out, and then they were at the next nearest community. On a main street they stopped and Dude and Dan looked around discreetly, to make sure no one was around. The others instinctively looked around attempting to look inconspicuous but failing instantly. There were very few people to be seen, and Dude whispered, "Come," and went down a side street with Dan. The others quickly followed.

To the backs of the buildings were wooden out houses. Having passed a few, Dude stopped at one. It was at this point that Joe realised that he had not been to the bathroom since he had arrived, and wondered if he should. He found he had absolutely no urge to make use of a toilet. They took another look around and then Dude opened the door and went in followed by Dan, who beckoned the rest of them in.

The outhouse was only big enough for one person, but they went in one after the other. When Joe looked inside, instead of a floor there were steep stairs spiraling down. A secret entrance! Joe was transported back to schoolboy adventures, and this was an adventure that he was eager to get to the end of.

They went down what felt like a hundred feet before the stairs stopped at the entrance to a tunnel.

"Wow that's fucking long," said Lilly. The tunnel was straight and the lights disappeared into the distance, and it was just wide enough to walk two abreast, and tall enough to walk upright. The supports were spaced precisely, with wooden planks lining the walls and ceiling.

"So, this tunnel leads to Jesus?" asked Joe.

"Yes man, this is his secret entrance," said Dude.

"I remember the tunnel before," said Isaiah. "It was not so impressive as this."

"Now y' can't go tellin' anybody about this," said Dan as they walked. "This is a big secret we're letting you in on."

"Jesus built this?" asked Joe.

"For real," said Dude.

"I thought he was a carpenter, not a civil engineer," said Joe.

"He had time," said Dan. "You can learn anything with enough time. Plus, I'm not all that sure he was a carpenter."

"When did he do this?" asked Isaiah.

"A few centuries ago," said Dan. "The old tunnel

became too short, and he was coming out of it in the middle of the crowd. People get pretty upset if they think you're jumping the queue. Especially if they've been in it for a few years. On top of that some were curious and found the entrance.

"It really was getting hard for him to get out of the house. All his other methods weren't working either. Shit the man got some skills, though. Jesus built this tunnel long after you went to the fields."

When they finally reached the tunnel's end there was another staircase. As they climbed the stairs Joe's curiosity was driving him on.

At the top of the stairs there appeared to be a stone slab. Dude lifted and pushed the slab aside.

They walked up into a room with stone walls and wooden beams on the ceiling, with the underside of the palm leaves that thatched the roof visible. Despite the ancient look of the walls' construction, they appeared fresh, and the windows were made of glass.

The area they had entered was open planned with the kitchen connected to another room by a wide, open section of wall. The shelves looked modern and there were things on the shelves that went from the distant past, to items he would have expected in a modern home. In the corner was a cooker made of stone, with an open front for the fuel and metal plates on top, covering holes where the heat would be used to cook. Hanging off hooks on the walls were a variety of pans and utensils. In a far corner was a fridge freezer.

When Joe looked closer at the windows, he noticed the glass was several layers thick. Joe looked out of the window, he thought he could see the tops of the observation towers in the distance. He saw crowds behind a fence, which Joe guessed to be several hundred metres away. There was a sudden surge of cheering and shouting from the crowd, which Joe could easily hear despite the dampening of the noise by the windows. Dan yanked Joe away. "Stay away from the windows," he said.

A screaming figure came charging through the open wall, wielding a three-wood golf club. "You better put down whatever you've got and get out, or I'm calling the demons!" he shouted, and stopped when he recognised Dude, Dan, and Isaiah. He smiled and spread out his arms, lowering the golf club, and exclaimed, "Dude! Dan! Isaiah!" He was dark skinned, clean shaven, had smartly cut short hair and wore a golf shirt and shorts, with what Joe thought looked like designer sandals.

Dude, Dan and Isaiah gave the man a hug one after the other. The man looked to Joe, Lilly and Kal. "So who are these chaps?" asked the man in an accent that sounded like he'd come out of a very British public school. Then he looked worried, "They did come with you, didn't they?" he asked.

"Man," said Dude appearing offended. "Y' can't be askin' that o' me."

"Of course," said the golfer. "What was I thinking?"

Dude turned to the two dumb struck humans and the incredibly intrigued alien, with its bright colours ily rotating, and its eyes and sensors flicking back and forth.

"Joe, Lilly 'n' Kal this is Jesus. Jesus meet Joe, Lilly 'n' Kal," said Dude.

End of Part One of Stoned In The Afterlife:
A Possible Journey.